SOUL OF GLASS

MEGAN O'RUSSELL

Ink Worlds Press

Visit our website at www.MeganORussell.com

This book is a work of fiction. Names, characters, places, and incidents either are products of the author's imagination or are used fictitiously. Any resemblance to actual persons, living or dead, events, or locales is entirely coincidental.

Soul of Glass

DEDICATION

For those who are brave enough to trust

SOUL OF GLASS

CHAPTER ONE

The cold of the water sank into my feet, chilling my whole body. My shoulders shook, and goose bumps covered my arms. But I couldn't bring myself to leave the creatures swimming just below me.

With only the moonlight and the soft glow of the tanks breaking the darkness, the silhouetted animals looked like demons or ghosts. The stingrays that swam in slow circles were the spirits of all the people who'd died in service to the domes, sacrificing their lives so the chosen few could wait out the apocalypse in paradise.

A sea turtle surfaced near my feet, taking in a breath of perfectly filtered air before sinking back below the water. The animal was massive and beautiful. In the daylight, I could watch the turtles swim for hours, weaving around the stingrays like life trapped in glass was the most natural thing in the world.

In the dark, even the sea turtles weren't enough to bring me joy. Or, not even joy. Just a resigned gratitude for my survival.

At night, the turtles were just cursed creatures clawing their way through the ghosts of the dead as they circled in purgatory until it was their turn to die.

I shut my eyes and pressed my hands to the metal grating of the walkway I sat on.

The air vents hummed as they brought in the filtered air. The pumps hummed as they circulated the water for the dozens of massive tanks housing everything from starfish to sharks. The gentle sound of waves lapping came from the far side of the dome.

There were no sirens or screams.

No racket of factory machines.

The air smelled of fish and salt without any hint of smoke or human filth tainting the scent.

"I am lucky," I whispered to myself. "I am lucky."

I lifted my feet out of the watery cell the turtles and stingrays shared, letting them drip for a moment before standing on the walkway that reached over the tops of the tanks.

I didn't bother putting on my still-shiny boots as I headed toward the far side of the dome. Inside the glass, everything was pristine. There wouldn't be anything on the path to hurt me.

How could there be? The domes wouldn't be paradise if I got a splinter in my foot.

I stopped at the top of the staircase on the far side of the tanks. Even after more than a month of living in the Arcadia Domes, I still had trouble believing the beach was real.

Sand stretched from one side of the glass to the other. The water beyond reached all the way to the edge of the dome. If I'd known how to swim, I could have dove down into the pool and swum over the reefs and fish. I could have hidden from everyone. Just floated below the surface, staring out at the world beyond the glass.

In my head, I knew the Incorporation's marine biologists used the pool in their research. Just like they used the animals in the tanks in their research.

But I couldn't make the beach feel useful or worth whatever sacrifices its creation had demanded.

If the Incorporation had decided to use their resources feeding the starving people in the cities instead of hauling sand and reefs up to the mountains—

"I am lucky. I am lucky."

I turned my gaze up to the moon peering in through the glass. The moon was almost full, bright enough I could only see a few stars scattered across the sky. It was still more than I'd been able to see through the shroud of smoke and constant glow of the city lights back home.

I tried to make myself enjoy the soft silver gleam drifting into the dome. The Incorporation hadn't created the moon, or trapped the stars. The kep had nothing to do with the night sky.

But the way the moon peered down through the glass, like it was watching me, made some childish part of me feel like I was the animal trapped in a tank, doomed to swim in circles until I died.

"I am lucky. I am lucky."

I headed back across the walkway toward the tunnels that linked the Arcadia Domes together.

"I am lucky."

The feeling of being watched scratched across the back of my neck. I shifted my boots to my left hand, instinctively reaching for the knife I knew damn well I didn't have.

I froze, listening for footsteps, or the pop of a kep gun shooting a dart into my neck. But the only sound was the hum of the domes maintaining their perfection.

I looked back up to the moon. "Stare all you want. I'll be right here until I die."

The weight of all the water in the tanks seemed to press on my chest, drowning me in the certainty that I was a shit for not being grateful for everything I had.

"I am lucky."

Whispering the words over and over didn't lift the weight

from my chest as I went down the stairs and into the concrete corridor that cut through the earth and led to the other domes.

Only one guard walked by—a woman who pursed her lips at the boots I still carried in my hand. I gave her a shy smile and kept walking.

I should have been more careful to seem happy and normal. To laugh and revel in every luxury my new home had to offer.

I would have shattered the domes to protect my little sister, and I wouldn't have grieved for the lives lost. But I couldn't make myself feel joy for her sake.

Maybe that part of me is just broken.

Shadows filled Bloom Dome as I walked up the stairs into the place Mari and I now called home. Dim lights shone from the edges of the tree-lined path, casting their glow onto the delicate flowers the birds feasted on during the day.

The scent of cherry blossoms filled the air as I crept toward our building. I took deep breaths, trying to let the scent calm me.

"I have Mari. I have food and water. I have a home. I am lucky."

Careful not to crush any of the blooms, I stepped through the flowerbed that surrounded our building, ignoring the front door and slipping around to the side of the housing unit.

The thin strip of metal waited right where I'd tucked it, inside a cluster of flowers with pale purple petals.

It took less than a minute for me to slip the metal into the side of the window and jimmy open the lock. I slid the window up and waited for a moment, listening for any sounds of fear.

Nothing. Just darkness and peace.

I climbed through the window and into the room I shared with Mari. She didn't even stir as I closed the window and fastened the lock back into place.

With her black hair splayed around her and her face relaxed in a serenity people like us weren't meant to know, my little sister looked like a girl in a story—sound asleep, waiting for a fairy to come whisk her away on a grand adventure.

We're so lucky.

I tucked the strip of metal under my mattress and checked the chair I'd jammed against our door. Everything was secure and safe.

I sat at the table, waiting for fatigue I knew wouldn't come.

CHAPTER TWO

"The primary goal of each of our departments is to serve the mission of the Incorporation," Mrs. Hale said. "Just as serving the mission of the Incorporation must be the focal point in each of our lives."

I pressed my hands flat against my desk, concentrating on keeping my face passive and my gaze to the front of the room where Mrs. Hale had pulled up a flow chart of each of the departments in the domes. There were big circles for things like Outer Guard, Dome Guard, Plant Preservation, Medical, Animal Husbandry, and Maintenance, and smaller circles for things like Transportation, Veterinary Care, Genetic Research, Education, and Asset Management.

"As citizens of the Arcadia Domes, we have the privilege and responsibility of serving the mission of the Incorporation in every aspect of our lives. It's my privilege and responsibility to teach all of you, to educate you on our history, the sciences that help us survive, and yes"—Mrs. Hale looked to one of the boys in the front row—"the math behind those sciences. But the most vital lesson I need to be sure you carry with you for the rest of your lives is our duty to the future.

"The domes weren't built to keep *us* alive and comfortable. They were built for the ones who will come generations after us. In everything we do, we must consider those who have yet to be born. Refusing to learn the material I'm giving you today will leave less knowledge to be passed on to future generations."

The bell marking the end of the school day dinged.

"Which is why I expect all of your work for tomorrow to be pristine. Enjoy your evening."

The others in the class all grabbed their tablets and headed toward the door.

I lifted my palms from my desk. My arms ached from having pressed down so hard for so long. I tested my temper, making sure I had the willpower to not throw my tablet before lifting it off my desk. I started to leave, following the rest of the class.

"Lanni," Mrs. Hale said loudly enough I couldn't ignore her.

One of the students' shadows stopped at the bottom of the stairs.

"Yes, Mrs. Hale?" I pressed a careful smile onto my face as Mrs. Hale stepped around me, blocking my escape route.

"I just wanted to take a moment to check in with you." Mrs. Hale furrowed her brow in a concerned sort of way. "How are you doing?"

"Fine." I gripped my tablet. "I think I've been keeping up with your assignments."

"Oh, absolutely. I've been very pleased with your work."

"Thank you." I gave her a nod and stepped to the side, hoping to skirt around her.

"I'm more concerned about you as a person than as a student." Mrs. Hale stepped sideways, blocking my path again.

I glanced toward the stairs.

Five corridors to reach the Herd Dome. One minute to stash Mari in the paddocks, then...

I don't know how we'd get out.

"Most of my students have been in the same class since they

started school," Mrs. Hale said. "For better or worse, they know each other very well. You and Walsh coming in so close to the end of your education can't be easy."

"I'm really fine," I said.

"I've been impressed with how Walsh has integrated with the other students."

An ember of rage burned in my gut.

"But you still seem to be all on your own," Mrs. Hale said.

"I have to take care of my little sister."

"She can't be your whole world, Lanni." Mrs. Hale placed her hand on my shoulder.

"Yes, she can." Every nerve in my body begged me to shove her away.

"It seems like that now, but in the long term, making friends will be better for you and Mari. Which is one of the reasons you'll be getting some extra assignments." Mrs. Hale's brow smoothed as she smiled.

"What kind of assignments?"

"PAM will give you all the details. I just wanted you to know in advance that this isn't a punishment. I care about your future, and I believe you can thrive. Think of this as my way of helping you secure a joyous and bountiful life."

"Thanks." I tucked my chin and rounded my shoulders enough to break away from Mrs. Hale's hand.

"Go see to your sister." Mrs. Hale winked. "You're an amazing girl, Lanni. You deserve a chance at happiness."

I gripped my tablet hard enough to hurt my fingers as I headed down the steps. The shadow that had waited in the stair-well slipped away before I reached him.

Walsh didn't have the courtesy to bolt or even pretend he'd been tying his boot as I stepped out into the corridor. He just met my gaze and walked away, like he wanted to be sure I knew he'd been eavesdropping but was too much of a coward to stick around so I could say anything about it.

Not that I would have. Ours was a fragile peace, and I couldn't risk shattering it.

It had been a month of him lingering nearby, eavesdropping on me. Or waiting until we had a bunch of classmates around us, then laying his hand on my shoulder and saying nice things about how glad he was to have someone from the Ice Domes with him. How I was a piece of home.

Like I could have forgotten the lie I'd been trapped in.

If I'd only had to worry about myself, I would have told him to leave me the hell alone. But I couldn't risk him outing me. If the Incorporation figured out I hadn't been born in the domes and wasn't really a kep, they'd know Mari didn't belong, either. Then we'd both be kicked out of the Arc Domes. Or worse. I didn't know if the Incorporation would execute children or if they'd prefer to keep their hands clean and just toss us outside to slowly die.

I dug my fingers into my hair, pulling hard on the roots as I walked toward Mari's classroom. It didn't stop me from wanting to punch Walsh in the face, but it made the anger zinging through my arms settle enough that I could shake out my shoulders and unclench my jaw before I turned down the corridor to the Herd Dome.

Mari waited at the bottom of the steps, bouncing on her toes as she spoke to two other girls from her class.

"—just the fluffiest thing I've ever seen," Sarah said.

"But I don't like the way the wool feels." Ellie wrinkled her nose.

"I love all the animals," Mari said. "But the donkey is definitely my favorite."

I bit back my laugh as I stopped beside the girls.

"You're late." Mari took my hand.

"I had to stay a little after class," I said.

"Why?" Mari wrinkled her forehead.

"To talk to my teacher about a new assignment." I winked,

trying to make it seem like I'd been granted a fun project instead of a fresh reason to worry.

"It's okay," Ellie said. "We waited with her."

"Thanks. Come on, Mar. Let's get you fed." I waved to the girls and led Mari toward Bloom Dome.

"I got to feed animals in the Herd Dome today." Mari pranced along beside me. "We got to help groom them, too. And not just the sheep and donkeys. Has your class been in the Herd Dome?"

"Nope."

"Well, they have little animals, too." Mari took a shuddering breath like she was bracing herself for the most miraculous thing. "They have rabbits, *real* rabbits, and cows, and goats..."

She kept the list going all the way up the stairs to Bloom Dome and along the tree-lined path to our building.

I let go of her hand to open the main door.

"And the best part is we get to go back twice more this week," Mari said. "And the teacher said we'll get to keep going back all year."

"That's amazing, Mar."

A box of food waited outside the door to our room. A whole box of food just sitting in the hallway.

I picked it up as Mari opened our door.

"And there are some grownups whose whole job is just to take care of the animals in the Herd Dome." Mari kicked off her boots and ran through the kitchen to throw herself onto her bed. "That's really their whole, entire job. They feed them, and take care of them, and clean up after them, which would be smelly, but I don't think I'd mind."

"So you want to work in the Herd Dome?" I didn't open the box of food. I just set it on the counter before closing the door, taking off my boots and walking to my bed. I didn't realize what I'd done until I sat down opposite Mari.

"I don't know yet," Mari said. "Because there are people who work on flowers all day, too."

I'd been given a treasure, and I hadn't even looked at it. Like knowing I'd be able to feed Mari wasn't a wonder I needed to appreciate. People would have been willing to kill for that box in the city.

I'm becoming a kep.

"...or a doctor maybe."

I blinked, trying to catch up to Mari's words.

"I'd like to help people." Mari pursed her lips. "But I think I'll have to see how many explosions the doctors here get patients from."

"You have plenty of time to figure it out." I set my tablet on the table. Another wonder no one in the city could have hoped to possess.

Except Mari and me. Amery made sure we'd have a tablet and a way to learn. We had to be ready to come here. Had to be ready to pretend to be everything we're not.

"Are you okay?" Mari crossed the few feet between our beds to sit beside me.

"Of course I am." I kissed the top of Mari's head. "My brain is just tired from packing in so much schoolwork."

"Then you should rest. I'll make us dinner."

"Mar—"

"They also have people who make sure everyone gets the right amount of food." Mari skipped to the counter. "Feeding everyone could be fun, too."

I dug my knuckles into my eyes until white spots danced in my vision.

My tablet dinged.

I pulled it off the table and lay down on my bed.

A little tab in the corner showed a message from PAM.

Schedule addition to begin tomorrow evening.

Class assignment.

Elder-focused learning opportunity. Meet in the atrium at 6 p.m.

Assignment partners: Gideon Pace and Mr. Travis Lewis

CHAPTER THREE

I didn't eat at all the next day. I just couldn't manage to get my stomach to stop shaking long enough to accept food. It was ridiculous.

Not very long ago, I had been living in our apartment in the city. Not very long ago, the concept of refusing fresh fruit, vegetables, and meat would have been completely absurd.

But now, I lived in the domes with the kep. Food would appear at my door every day. So much food that Mari and I had to stuff ourselves to finish it.

I'd made myself stare at the food I was wasting and picture the desperate people it could have fed back home and how much Jaime could have made from trading it. But knowing I was wrong for not eating it didn't make me feel any better. It only made me more nauseous.

Sitting in class, my hands sweat so badly, I had to keep wiping them on my pants so I didn't drop my tablet.

I searched Mrs. Hale's face for some hint that my *not punishment* extra assignment was actually a ploy for them executing Mari and me for sneaking into the Arc Domes. But she only smiled at me and winked.

Part of me wished I had warned Mari to hide in case the guards came to haul her away, but I couldn't risk putting her on edge and having people find out something was wrong in case nothing was actually wrong. But if I had been told to go to the atrium so I could be publicly executed, then not warning Mari might have doomed her, too.

The horrible loop of doubt swirled around and around in my head, making it impossible for me to focus on anything Mrs. Hale said.

Our class moved from our normal room to the Haven Dome for our afternoon lesson.

They kept us in a pack as we traveled from one place to the other. Everyone around me chatted and laughed. I gripped my tablet, just trying to look calm.

"Lanni." Walsh weaved between people to walk beside me. "You okay?"

I gripped my tablet hard enough I was amazed it didn't crack.

"Of course." I pressed a smile onto my face. "Haven Dome is one of my favorites. Not the most exotic, but I like knowing I've actually worked with some of the plants I eat."

"You sure?" Walsh put a hand on the back of my waist, steering me out of the stream of students.

"Why are you touching me?" I tried to keep the tension out of my shoulders.

"Old friends look out for each other, Lanni." Walsh kept his hand on my waist, walking slowly enough to drop us behind the rest of the pack.

"What does that mean?"

"Something's making you panic."

"I don't know what you—"

"What hurts you hurts me, too." Walsh nodded to two guards as they passed.

They both had full gear on—weapons, helmets, vests, jackets. I hoped that meant they were leaving the domes. The helmets would have been overkill if all they were planning was an execution in the atrium.

"So what is it?" Walsh said.

"Don't you already know? You spy on me enough."

I'd expected Walsh to deny it, but he only grinned. "Even I can't watch you all the time."

"You're such an ass."

We reached the stairs that led up into the Haven Dome.

"Tell me what it is, or I'll have to find out for myself." Walsh let go of my waist as we reached the top of the stairs.

There weren't any tables or planting trays laid out. The students had all lined up in the rows of crops that reached toward the glass.

"I have a new assignment," I said. "I'm supposed to go to the atrium at six. If they know—"

"Don't." Walsh squeezed my shoulder. "The atrium is nothing to worry about. Just go, and play nice."

"How do you know?" A tiny bit of the fear knotted in my chest loosened. I hated myself for believing him.

"You're not the only one I watch." He stepped away from me to stand with two of the girls in our class. Both of them blushed like they were honored to have been chosen.

I made my way to the very end of the line, where I had a clear view through the glass.

Just outside the dome, the mountain dropped away, offering a perfect view of the soaring peaks of the surrounding mountains and the unblemished forest below.

I made myself breathe slowly, keeping my gaze fixed on the view, trying to convince myself that punching Walsh was not an option. Neither was running.

"Good afternoon, class." Mrs. Burton, the teacher who worked with our class for our practical botany lessons, walked between the two rows of students. "We have an abundance of peppers growing in this dome, and today you are going to help me harvest them and prep the food for distribution."

A general sigh of resignation floated from the class.

"I hate peppers," the boy nearest me whispered to the student on his other side. "We should just trash them all so no one has to eat them."

The other student gave a quiet laugh.

I fixed my gaze on the plants in front of me. Pick the peppers, put them on a cart, send them down to distribution. Easy tasks. Not that different from being on the factory floor.

It couldn't be more different. Jaime's voice echoed in my head. *That doesn't mean you can't survive it.*

Everything went blurry for the rest of the lesson.

The other students talked and laughed while they worked. Mrs. Burton didn't mind. Every once in a while, she'd warn the students not to talk with their hands, but there were no raised voices or punishments threatened if a student fell behind the group's pace as we harvested.

I would have been denied my water ration if I'd fallen behind on the factory floor. I could have died just because I hadn't worked fast enough.

I couldn't make the differences mesh together in my mind. Luxury and laughter should not exist in a world where Death hides in the shadows, just waiting for his chance to strike.

I read each of the signs painted on the walls on my way home. I'd memorized all of them my first week inside, but I still read them. Having something to focus on made being in the tunnels easier.

It wasn't being underground that set my nerves on edge every time I walked the concrete corridors. It was not being able to see what lurked in front of me.

The halls all had a gentle arc to them, like they'd been built to match the curves of the mountain's slopes. I suppose it made sense to build everything that way, but if you looked too far ahead or behind, all you could see was concrete walls with no way to know if enemies were racing toward you from just out of sight.

I made Mari dinner—steamed vegetables and grains—but I still couldn't eat.

I couldn't trust Walsh. I didn't even know if Connor Walsh was actually his name.

Mari had already started her homework before I had to leave for the atrium. She just smiled when I kissed her head and left.

I leaned against the wall in the hall of our building. Harper lived a few doors down from us. Part of me wanted to knock on her door and ask her to hide Mari until I was certain my assignment in the atrium wasn't just a way to get me to walk to my own execution. But there would be no way to hide Mari from the kep, not in the long term. And scaring Mari would only make things worse if Walsh had told me the truth and I really was freaking out about nothing.

"Get your shit together, Lanni," I whispered to myself. "You've been through too much to fall apart now."

I twisted my hair into a bun as I headed toward the atrium, just so I would have something to do with my hands as I walked through the corridors and up the three sets of stairs it took to reach the highest of the Arc Domes' levels.

I'd only been up to the atrium twice before. Once on my second day inside, when our guardian Miranda had taken us on a tour, and once a week later, when I'd started hunting for places to hide and possible escape routes.

I'd searched all the areas I was allowed to enter, looking for an emergency exit or an air vent we might be able to climb through, just in case the kep came after us. Or in case the people who'd blown up the depot targeted the Arc Domes. Or in case Walsh decided to out us as intruders in this perfect world of glass and plenty.

But in the end, it didn't matter how many ways everything could go horribly wrong. I hadn't managed to find an escape route, let alone a plan to keep Mari safe if we had to run from a mob of angry, armed kep.

"Hey, Lanni," a voice called from behind as I climbed the last flight of stairs to the atrium.

I tensed as I turned toward the voice.

One of the boys from my class bounded up the steps behind me, smiling like he was thrilled to see me.

"Hi," I said as the boy reached me.

"Do you have any idea what Mr. Lewis looks like?" The boy brushed aside his chestnut-brown hair, which had flopped across his forehead.

"Nope." I kept climbing the stairs.

"Any idea what we're supposed to be doing?"

We're.

Gideon Pace.

I looked at the boy, trying to remember the teachers having called him by name.

"I only know that PAM told me to come to the atrium," I said.

"Well, maybe he'll be holding a sign." The boy I thought was probably Gideon shrugged. "Either that or this is going to get really awkward."

A small but genuine laugh shook a bit of my panic away.

"Hopefully, he'll know what we're supposed to be doing," probably-Gideon said.

We reached the top of the stairs and stepped up into the atrium together.

It didn't matter that I'd seen it before. My feet still forgot how to move as awe and loathing washed over me.

A forest. That's what the Incorporation had created. An actual forest.

People sat on the moss surrounding the trees that were big enough to be a hundred years old. Benches had been placed in shadowy corners, perfect for private conversations. A pond filled with fish was surrounded by a pack of mothers trying to entertain their children. A many-branched stream, complete with three footbridges, ran through it all.

When my feet finally figured out they should be moving, they headed toward the glass without me asking them to. The sun had begun to set on the far side of the mountain, and, even though I couldn't see the sun itself, the colors of the sky smothered the rest of my panic, just for a moment. Like there wasn't enough of me to take in the beauty and think about all the ways things could go wrong at the same time.

Up above us, the Incorporation Headquarters glimmered in the fading light like fiery jewels that wanted to set the world on fire. Those smaller domes stretched toward the summit of the mountain, peeking out of the slope.

"It's beautiful, isn't it?" probably-Gideon said.

"It really is." I dug my nails into my palms, trying to distract myself from the awful feeling of being too small to have a hope of protecting Mari.

"Mr. Pace. Miss Roberts." An elderly man toddled toward us, his hand trailing along the glass. "So, you're the two saps they've stuck with me?"

CHAPTER FOUR

Travis Lewis was the oldest person I'd ever seen.

He had wispy, white hair, but it didn't look like it had fallen out in patches as some illness took over his body. It was more like his hair had worn away on top, like a spot on the floor that had been stood on too often.

Mr. Lewis had wrinkles on his face, like the older people in the city, but the wrinkles had spread all the way down to his hands. So when he reached forward to grasp my hand in greeting, his skin felt a little bit loose.

"It's a pleasure to meet you both, I'm sure." Mr. Lewis's jowls jiggled as he nodded.

"The pleasure is ours." Gideon shook Mr. Lewis's hand.

I opened my mouth to ask how old he was but managed to save myself midcourse. "How often do you meet with students?"

Mr. Lewis laughed and beckoned us to follow him.

I looked to Gideon, but he just shrugged. We stayed side by side, carefully keeping behind Mr. Lewis as he led us around the edge of the atrium.

"Do you know how much planning it took to create the domes?" Mr. Lewis asked.

"Years," Gideon said. "It was well over a decade between the announcement of the construction and the first dome being sealed."

"The planning began long before the announcement," Mr. Lewis said.

We reached the end of the stream that flowed through the atrium. The water didn't gather in a pool or tumble over a waterfall. It just stopped. Something had to be pulling the water underground, probably recirculating it to be run down the stream again.

A strip of mossy ground separated the unnatural end of the water from the glass of the dome. I wanted to dig down into the dirt and see how big the machines were that kept the stream running so the kep could have a pleasing place to relax.

Mr. Lewis stopped at a pair of benches nestled between two trees with deep red leaves.

"Sit, sit." He waved at one bench while carefully lowering himself onto the other.

I fought the urge to reach forward and help him. He was as unsteady as my mother had been the last time I'd seen her.

A pinch in my chest shoved the air out of my lungs.

"I don't bite." Gideon slid to one side of the bench we were to share.

"You don't scare me." I forced a smile onto my face and sat beside him.

Mr. Lewis's lips were moving. I could see them forming words, but I couldn't bring myself close enough to reality to hear the sound.

The pain in my chest sent me back to our dingy apartment and the lines for the water tanks. If the water tanks were still running, would Mom even be strong enough to carry a jug of water home? Would Amery take care of her, or had the father I'd never known abandoned her as soon as he'd shipped Mari and me far away?

Gideon laughed beside me. The sound of it, so easy and happy, snapped me back into the moment.

"The day we had to argue over how many pairs of boots we would need stockpiled and what sizes"—Mr. Lewis flapped a hand in the air—"I almost stormed away and never came back."

"How did you figure out how many pairs of boots you'd need?" Gideon asked.

"A wickedly complicated and probably unnecessary mathematical formula. After considering the average lifespan of a pair of normal citizen's boots, versus the wear of a Dome Guard's or, even worse, an Outer Guard's, then looking at the possibility of reissuing boots that weren't fully worn through when a citizen passed or outgrew them, then accounting for the probable genetic variations that might affect foot size in the future"—Mr. Lewis leaned forward like he was telling us a secret—"we made a very well-educated guess."

Gideon laughed again.

"But in all the things we accounted for, all the massive lists we created so generations could live inside the glass without wanting for anything," Mr. Lewis said, "we didn't account for aging."

"How do you mean?" I asked. "Do they not have enough supplies for the older people?"

"We have plenty of supplies," Mr. Lewis said. "And housing units set aside, and medical care prepared for the geriatric population, but we never considered what would happen once a citizen became too old to work. I have everything I need in my home. I could live for years only stepping outside my door to accept my food rations."

I gripped the bench, trying to anchor myself to the atrium instead of sliding back to the city. To the wounds in my life I could do nothing to mend.

"The ability to stay in one's house creates a lot of time for being lonely," Mr. Lewis said. "We never planned for that possibility. Though, I suppose pairing the older crowd with students for a visit once in a while is a nice solution, at least for me."

"For us, too," Gideon said. "I'm ashamed to admit it, sir, but other than what I've been taught in school, I don't actually know much about the early days of the domes."

"Saying it like that makes me feel even older." Mr. Lewis laughed.

"I'm sorry, sir," Gideon said.

"You're lucky to be so old," I said. "Not many people get to experience it."

Gideon froze beside me, but Mr. Lewis only laughed harder.

"Well said, Miss Roberts." Mr. Lewis looked up toward the Incorporation Headquarters right above our heads. "It's a pity they don't tell students what it was like when the glass was first sealed. There were problems, of course. It took time to get everyone accustomed to the idea of never leaving our tiny piece of the world. We all knew what we were signing up for. But, giving up the lives we'd known to protect future generations was a larger sacrifice than I think any of us truly understood."

"I am very grateful for the sacrifices you made," Gideon said.

I gripped the front of the bench so hard I thought my fingers might break.

"We did find some ways to make it easier." Mr. Lewis pointed toward the middle of the atrium. "I'm not sure you'll believe me, but we used to have dances right over there."

"Really?" Gideon asked.

"The speakers we use for announcements are capable of playing music. It wasn't anything fancy, just a get together every month or so. Something to look forward to. A way to mark the passage of time." Mr. Lewis swayed as though he could hear music in his head. "Went on for about the first five years. Most of the couples who married during that time can thank those dances for lighting the first spark."

"Why did the dances stop?" Gideon said.

Because the kep decided murdering city scum was more fun.

"An illness came," Mr. Lewis said. "Gathering was forbidden to help slow the spread. The woman who used to choose the music died. Dozens died. By the time it was safe for everyone to be together again, no one seemed to want to dance anymore."

"I'm so sorry," Gideon said.

"It's a small thing," Mr. Lewis said. "The salvation of the human race is certainly worth giving up dancing."

It went on like that for two hours.

Mr. Lewis would tell us a story. Gideon would ask questions while seeming absolutely in awe of how wonderful the original kep were for choosing to seal themselves inside the glass. I would try not to scream that not getting to dance in their fancy, manmade, fucking forest wasn't a real sacrifice.

The thousands upon thousands of people the Incorporation had worked to death in their factories, or killed when they rebelled, or just let starve to death in the streets—those people had sacrificed their lives so the kep could have enough boots to wait a few hundred years for the environment to get its shit together.

And no one had ever asked any of the factory rats if they wanted to die so the kep could have a fancy stream that disappeared into the ground.

That's not sacrifice. It's murder.

I kept a smile on my face and tried to listen closely enough to ask Mr. Lewis questions. But the pinching in my chest turned into a fist squeezing my heart.

Murderer. I wanted to scream the word at Mr. Lewis and throw him into the stream, see if the machines that dragged the water down could tear through an evil man's body.

When Mr. Lewis finally freed us, I shook his hand again. I didn't want to touch him. His hands should have been slicked with innocent blood. Their cleanliness was an abomination, another piece of Incorporation propaganda.

I tucked my hands into my pockets as I headed home, trying to hide their trembling as I fought the urge to scream.

"Lanni, wait up," Gideon called before I reached the stairs.

I slowed my steps enough for him to catch up to me.

"That wasn't the worst thing." He matched my pace down the stairs.

"I guess not," I said.

"Honestly, when I saw the message from PAM, I thought we'd be on some weird cleanup duty."

"Do you get a lot of evening assignments here?"

"Hated spending time with me that much?" Gideon nudged me with his elbow.

"No, I just…"

Don't scream. Don't scream.

"I have to take care of my sister."

"Right." Gideon froze. "I'm so sorry."

I stopped three stairs down. "It's fine. Mari can be alone for a few hours."

"No, I mean, I forgot." Gideon dragged his fingers through his floppy, chestnut hair. "I forgot you two were on your own. That was really awful of me. I apologize."

"It's fine." I nodded for him to keep walking with me. "I can take care of Mari on my own. It's just easier for me if I'm with her."

"I get it. I mean, not really, I'm sure. But if I only had one person left, I don't think I'd ever want them out of my sight."

"Yeah." The shaking in my hands eased just a tiny bit.

"Well, if they schedule us for another meeting with Mr. Lewis, maybe you can bring your sister along." Gideon hurried down a few stairs to walk beside me. "I don't think he'd mind a larger audience."

CHAPTER FIVE

Thousands of people living trapped inside the glass...and I've never felt so alone.

I knew what I was agreeing to when I accepted this assignment. I knew the risks, and I knew the plan. Please don't think me weak when I say the isolation is worse than knowing I might die.

Every day, I see hundreds of people. I smile at them. I talk to them. As far as they know, I am one of them.

None of them see the demon walking their halls. That's the way it has to be.

If they found out what we have planned, we'd be done. We have one chance for success, and a single crack in the façade would be enough to shatter the future so many have died trying to create.

Every word I speak is a lie. Every smile I give is a threat.

It's stretching me apart from the inside out. I wonder how long it will be before there is nothing left of me and all that remains is the lie.

I am trying not to lose myself. I remind myself every day, every hour, that they are the enemy. They are not people. They are sheep, and I am the wolf come to slaughter them all.

When the time comes, I will know the names of the dead. I will know *which corpses should be burned together because they would not want to be separated even in death.*

I wish I didn't have to know these things. It would have been easier if they had remained a faceless enemy.

My duty is to play a role as I wander among the sheep, pretending I am an innocent member of the flock. But my fear grows every time I tear a little piece of myself away, offering bits of my soul to convince them my lies are true.

If there is nothing left of me when the battle begins, will I remember what part I was created to play? Or will I have lost enough of myself that I'll forget it is the sheep who are the real monsters?

See you in the embers,

~C

CHAPTER SIX

After Mr. Lewis and Gideon, I had an evening meeting with Mrs. Hunt and Lucas. Then I moved on to Mr. Marin and Elliot.

Gideon was never assigned another elderly kep to talk to.

Every time PAM notified me of another evening *assignment*, my gut would tighten. I tried to tell myself it was just because I hated leaving Mari and didn't want to spend my whole evening listening to a kep tell me how wonderful the domes were. But I couldn't really convince myself that was the whole reason I couldn't eat before the meetings.

I was the only one in my class always being called to the atrium. Mrs. Hale had said it wasn't a punishment, but I was unquestionably being singled out. And if whatever reason she had began to morph into suspicion, I didn't know how long Mari and I would last.

It was like I was living in a haze of panic. Feeling everyone's eyes watching me. Knowing that if I screwed up, I'd be risking Mari's life.

I made sure my schoolwork was perfect and our room immaculate. Mari's clothes were clean, and she always had her work done, too.

But I kept getting sent to the atrium, because it wasn't anything I was doing wrong. It was me.

Smile. Relax. Listen. Respond. Smile. Relax. Listen. Respond.

I'd repeat the words over and over as the elderly kep of the night told story after story about the early days of the domes, and I used every bit of self-control I had to keep from screaming that every good thing the kep had was bought with the blood of factory rats like me.

The people who made their boots, and glass, and syringes weren't animals to be used until they died. The factory rats were people with moms, and friends, and little sisters.

Then PAM dinged with a new notification.

Schedule addition to begin tomorrow evening.

Class assignment.

Elder-focused learning opportunity. Meet in the atrium at 6 p.m.

Assignment partners: Connor Walsh and Mr. Dominic Strand

From the time I woke up that morning, a horrible pressure tightened around my neck. Not like a knot in my throat. It went all the way around. I ignored it as I got Mari ready for school and dropped her off at her classroom.

I tried to swallow past the growing pain as I sat in class. We were working through math problems when I finally realized what the feeling was—a noose tightening around my neck, cutting off my air. And they would cut off my air. The kep would kill me and Mari as soon as they found out what I was.

The pain and pressure shifted down to my chest. I was failing Mari. My mother and Amery shouldn't have sent me away with her. They shouldn't have trusted me to take care of her.

"Hey."

The word yanked me out of my panicked thoughts.

Gideon was walking beside me. I didn't remember leaving the classroom. I didn't know where I was supposed to be going.

"Hey." My voice came out strange. Raw and raspy.

Get your shit together, Lanni.

"Are you okay?" Gideon kept pace beside me.

Walsh walked right in front of me with some of the other students, but I still had no idea where we were going.

"Lanni?" Gideon furrowed his brow.

"I haven't been sleeping," I said. "I think I'm still getting used to being here."

"Oh," Gideon said. "I'm sorry."

"It's fine." I forced the smile I hated back onto my face. "I'm just a little out of it."

"Well, I was thinking about the other night, when we were talking with Mr. Lewis, and—"

"Who's the guy we're talking to tonight?" Walsh took a step back to walk on my other side. "Strand, is it?"

"Yeah," I said.

"I hope he's interesting," Walsh said.

"It'll be great." I tried to brighten my smile.

"I've met Strand," Gideon said. "You'll like him. He has some epic stories."

"You love a good story." Walsh winked and took my hand, looping my arm through his. "I should come by and say hi to Mari tonight."

He draped his free hand over mine as I tensed.

"We can walk to the atrium together," Walsh said. "Take the time to get caught up."

"I know my way to the atrium," I said.

"But I haven't seen Mari in forever," Walsh said. "I'll swing by and get you."

I wanted to hit him. Right there in the middle of the hall. Just punch him and damn the consequences.

"She'll be happy to see you," I said.

"Great." Walsh smiled at me, one of his grins that held danger behind his charm, like a beautiful beast luring in its victim as it waited to pounce.

I wasn't sure if I was part of his trap or his prey.

I let him keep my arm through his as we went up the stairs into the Tropics Dome for a lesson on the importance of natural remedies. He led me toward the side of the class farthest from the teacher.

Gideon stayed on my other side as we started taking notes on which plants were prized for their anti-viral properties.

But when Walsh leaned close to whisper in my ear, not even Gideon could have heard.

"Breathe, Lanni. You've got to breathe."

Walsh took an exaggerated breath, filling his lungs all the way before exhaling slowly.

He gave me a nod, before taking another breath.

I tried to make my lungs expand, but the pressure on my chest only got worse. A rumble started in my ears, drowning out whatever the teacher was saying.

"You're okay." Walsh mouthed the words at me.

I took another breath.

He kept breathing with me, and the pressure in my chest and around my throat eased. The noise faded until I could hear the teacher's voice again. It only made me want to punch him in the jaw even more.

When the class finally ended, he just gave me a wink and a nod before walking away.

I kept my steps even as I hurried to the stairs, wanting to make sure I was well away from everyone in case the rumble came back and I completely fell apart like the failure I was.

"Lanni," Gideon called after me.

I pretended I couldn't hear him.

CHAPTER SEVEN

I drummed my fingers beside the screen set into the wall of our room, staring at the shining black rectangle, trying to decide if I was paranoid or not.

I tapped the button to call Miranda. The computer only dinged three times before our guardian appeared.

"Lanni," Miranda said my name like my calling was a welcome surprise. "How are you?"

"Fine." I took a breath. "I was wondering if Mari could come see you for a while tonight. I have an assignment in the atrium, and I don't want her spending the whole evening alone."

"Of course." Miranda nodded. Her brown curls bounced gently around her face like she'd grown them just to highlight her smile. "Send her on over. Did you want to eat dinner here, too?"

"No thanks. Can I come get her when I'm done?"

"Sure. See you soon."

"Thanks." I tapped the screen to turn it off.

"I'm fine here by myself," Mari said from her seat at our table.

"I know. But it'll be good for you to spend time with Miranda."

"She smiles a lot."

"I know."

"You don't."

I looked at Mari. "I do smile. I smile all the time."

"Not for real." Mari laid her tablet down on the table. "Are you okay?"

"Why does everyone keep asking me that?" I dug my nails into my palms.

"Because you don't look okay. Are you sick?"

"Of course not. We're in the domes, people don't get sick here."

"But you don't eat as much as you should. And you don't sleep. And your skin is getting paler. And you're getting skinnier. And I don't like any of it."

I started to say something funny about not liking all the dome food, but her eyes were wide, and tears shimmered in the corners.

"I don't want you to waste like Mom." Mari bit her lips together, like she was afraid she'd said something wrong. "If you're sick, you should go see the doctor. You can do that here."

I swallowed, making sure my throat could work before daring to speak. "I'm not sick, Mar. I'm just not as good at life here as you are."

"Yes, you are."

"I'm not."

"You could be." Mari got up and hugged me, pressing her cheek against my side. "You don't have to worry here. I know you have to take care of me, but I can take care of you, too. We're going to be okay."

"Thanks, Mar." I kissed the top of her head.

"But you have to eat." She took the apple from her dinner plate and pressed it into my hand. "You have to promise."

"I promise."

Mari glared at me until I took a bite of the apple.

The texture and sweetness of the fruit didn't seem real. I might as well have been chewing on a daydream.

"Go on over to Miranda's." I tried to hand her her tablet.

"I can stay here alone." Mari crossed her arms.

"If I send you to Miranda's, she'll be impressed that I'm asking for help and making sure you're supervised." I tucked Mari's tablet into her arms. "Seven-year-old kep don't stay at home by themselves. Go let her coo over you, and don't tell her I've been letting you stay here alone."

"You better eat that whole apple." Mari headed for the door.

"Be good, Mari," I called after her.

"Eat your dinner, Lanni," she called back.

A smile, a real, genuine smile, touched my lips before panic crushed my chest.

Mari was doing well in the domes. I couldn't let anyone ruin it for her.

I pulled one of the knives out of our kitchen drawer. The blade hadn't been made for fighting, but at least it had a sharp edge.

"What are you going to do with it, Lanni?" I whispered. "Where would you hide a body? You can't even find an escape route."

I put the knife back in the drawer and slammed it shut.

"You okay in there?" Walsh called from the hall.

I dragged my fingers through my hair, trying to smooth it out so I wouldn't look like I was losing my mind, before opening the door.

"Sounded like a cutlery drawer." Walsh leaned against my doorjamb. "Did one of the knives offend you?"

"The problem wasn't with the knife," I said.

"Where's Mari?" He peeked around me.

"Not here."

"Sent her away before I could see her? I even got here early so we could visit."

"Good thing I sent her away early then."

We stood in the doorway for a moment, both of us refusing to move.

"Are you ready to go now?" Walsh said. "There's something in the atrium I wanted to show you before our appointment with Mr. Strand."

"There's nothing you could show me that I'd want to see."

"Maybe." He shrugged. "But I definitely have some things you need to hear, and I think it would be better for us both to be out where we can be seen."

"What does that mean?"

"Finish your apple, and I'll tell you while we walk." He glanced at my waist. "And for your sake, don't try to stash a knife."

"Afraid I'll gut you?"

"Nope. Just looking out for you."

I took another bite of my apple and left the rest on the counter.

I wished I had grabbed a knife as I followed him down the hall.

He didn't speak again until we were outside and on the tree-lined path.

"You should have finished your apple."

"Do you want me to go back and get it for you?"

"Nope." He nudged his shoulder against mine. "It's time to see and be seen."

"What does that mean?" The itch of people watching me prickled the back of my neck.

"I'm not your enemy." Walsh nodded to a woman in a doctor's uniform.

The doctor nodded back.

"And why should I believe that?" I asked.

"Plenty of reasons." He turned to walk backward as he counted off on his fingers. "One, it's true. Two, I could have done plenty of damage by now if I'd wanted to. Three, you're not my enemy, so why should I be yours? Four, I have something very valuable to offer."

"What's that?" My fingers itched for a knife or a rock, anything to defend myself with.

He stopped at the top of the concrete stairs. "You'll have to wait. Hallways carry sound."

A child's cry flooded the stairwell as a man carried a screaming toddler up into Bloom Dome.

Part of me wondered if Walsh had somehow made the child cry just to prove his point.

We walked side by side down the stairs and through the corridors. Walsh kept his hands in his pockets, like he was relaxed and confident he wouldn't need his fists to fight. He kept humming to himself, not a full song, just a handful of notes at time, like he wasn't even meaning to make a sound and the tune just came out naturally.

"What song it that?" I asked when he went through the refrain for the sixteenth time.

"Do you know a lot of music?"

"No."

"Then you wouldn't know it." He stopped at the bottom of the stairs to the atrium. "Maybe someday I'll sing the whole song for you."

"No thanks." I started up the steps without him.

"Careful, Lanni. There might come a time when you'll regret rejecting my singing."

"Is that a threat?"

"Not at all." Walsh ran up a few stairs to walk beside me. "More like a hopeful premonition."

"You're such a—"

"Charming young man?" Walsh grinned.

I chewed my lips together, picturing Mari's face as I swallowed all the things I wanted to shout.

When we reached the top of the stairs, I went to turn right, toward the benches where I'd met the elders for the rest of my assignments.

"This way." Walsh headed left, toward the denser trees where the tiny branches of the stream all bubbled along as they flowed down to join the rest of the water.

He didn't stick to the path. He cut across the moss, weaving between trees. Before we'd traveled a hundred feet, I couldn't see anyone around us. Or anything really, besides the branches dripping with perfect green leaves and the foot-wide stream that gurgled as it raced between rocks.

Walsh turned in a slow circle, eyes closed and head tipped to the side. "Perfect. Have to be careful about couples sneaking around back here."

"I'd be more concerned with guards."

"A Dome Guard lurking in the trees just waiting to overhear us?" Walsh raised an eyebrow. "Not likely. The Incorporation values its citizens' right to privacy. Random spying isn't their style. The only security cameras in the Arc Domes watch the weapons locker, vehicle bay, and entrance to the Incorporation Headquarters. The only eyes and ears the Incorporation has in the atrium are human, and I haven't done anything suspicious enough to warrant a guard being assigned to trail me. Have you?"

"What do you want, Walsh?" I dug my nails into my palms.

"It's not what *I* want. It's what *you* need."

"What the hell is that supposed to mean?"

"You need to calm down, Lanni."

"You have no right to tell me to calm down." I leaned closer to Walsh. "You're half the reason I'm fucking panicking."

"I get it."

"You get needing to protect Mari?" I spoke through my teeth to keep from screaming. "You get having someone tell you they hold your life and your little sister's life in their hands and not knowing when they're going to decide they're sick of playing and just get you both killed? No, Connor Walsh. I don't think you do get it."

Walsh's face shifted. Softened. I don't really know how to describe it. It was like the only face I'd ever seen him wear was a mask, and the person beneath broke free for just a second.

"I would never out you or Mari." He took my hand and stepped closer to me so we were almost standing cheek to cheek. "I don't give a shit about anyone else in here. But you and Mari, you're not like them. You're innocent in all this. I'm sorry if I've made this harder on you. I didn't have a choice. Just know they will never find out about you from me. You have my word."

"Why should I believe you?"

"I want to make a trade." He laced his fingers through mine, leaning even closer so our cheeks brushed together. I didn't back away. "A truth for a truth."

"No."

"I'm not your enemy, Lanni."

"I don't know if I can." I closed my eyes.

"Why not?"

"A truth is a big thing to ask for."

He gave a soft laugh that rumbled in his chest. "Then I'll go first as a show of good faith. I can't turn you in, because I shouldn't be here, either. I don't belong in the glass. Someone made a hole in the domes' computer system to sneak you and Mari in. We found it. I was added to the database using the same flaw. You, me, Mari…we're all in the same boat. They find one of us, they find all three of us."

I pulled away enough to look at him. The softer face I'd seen before was gone, but there was only truth in his eyes.

"Your turn," he whispered.

"There's not a lot of truth that's mine to tell."

"Pity." He stepped away from me. The air around me suddenly seemed cold without his arm pressing against mine. "That wasn't even the thing you needed to know."

"I can't tell you how I got here. I can't even tell you where I'm from, not without putting people in danger."

"What sort of danger?"

"If someone finds out about us, I don't want to bring decent people down with me." I looked into the trees, just waiting for a guard to come storming through, gun drawn and aimed at my neck. "I don't want anyone to suffer because they helped Mari and me."

"I didn't think you'd be so sentimental about people from the domes." Walsh shifted sideways, making me look at him instead of the trees.

"Not all kep are equally evil."

"Huh. Shall we go meet Mr. Strand?" He took two steps away from me before I grabbed his arm.

"You haven't told me the thing I need to know yet."

"You're right. I haven't." He moved back toward me, not trying to get me to let go of his arm.

"Well, if we're in the same boat, don't you think I should have whatever information you have?"

"I already gave you something for nothing. I can't keep doing that."

"There's nothing I can tell you."

"Of course there is." Walsh took my free hand. "You're just not thinking hard enough."

My mind raced back to the start of it all. I lived in the city, but telling him where I'd come from implicated Harper and Alec. Being half-kep put Amery in danger, and even though I didn't give a shit about the father I'd never met, anyone finding out about Amery would definitely implicate Harper and Alec.

Everything else I knew didn't matter now that I'd been locked in the domes. My life was trapped in impenetrable glass, and the fact that I'd stolen syringes to sell was useless.

"One of the sets of domes fell," I whispered.

"You already told me that at the depot."

"I heard about it over a handheld radio. I don't know who was talking, I'd never picked up an actual signal before, but she said the domes had fallen. I think it must have been true. They'd been cracking down on the vampires where I was, and that night the kep lit the vampire district on fire, slaughtered the best workers they had. The guards wouldn't have done that unless they were afraid."

"Interesting." Walsh furrowed his bow, looking over my shoulder like he was reading something in the trees.

"But it wasn't the domes near me that fell." I squeezed his hand. "That means the signal came from far away. I can't be the only city scum in the world who managed to hear the news. Other people have got to know someone fought the domes and won."

Walsh slid his arm free from my grip. He touched my cheek, his thumb grazing my neck. "Never call yourself *city scum*, Lanni. Living outside the glass doesn't make you filthy or vile. It makes you stronger than the Incorporation understands."

I wanted to lean into his touch, to see if the warmth of his skin against mine would make me feel safer, even for a moment.

"Did I earn my truth yet?"

"Sure." He looked down at where our hands met. "You've got to settle in and make friends."

"What?" I pulled away from him.

"That's what these assignments are all about. Meeting new people."

"You can't be serious." I paced beside the tiny stream.

"Not just people. You've got to meet someone special."

"What's that supposed to mean?"

"Mrs. Hale has been sending you up here with every eligible young man in our class."

I froze. "You've got to be kidding me."

"Nope. She's playing matchmaker. You need a boyfriend."

"Why is my personal life any of her damn business?" I dug my fingers into my hair as I started pacing again. "What the hell does she think she's doing?"

"She's helping you adjust to your new home." Walsh tucked his hands into his pockets. "You haven't been making friends. You haven't been socializing. We're in a closed community. The only potential partners for you are locked inside the glass. Honestly, it's pretty nice of her to make sure you have a shot at finding someone who will make you happy."

"Happy? What would make me happy is being left alone."

"Which isn't going to happen. So you need to pick a guy and start dating him."

"Absolutely not."

"You don't have a choice, Lanni." Walsh stepped into my path. "You have to at least start to seem happy and well-adjusted."

"I get good grades. I take care of Mari."

"You look like a girl who's grieving."

"Maybe I am." I hated myself for saying it. I shouldn't have opened up that tiny tear in my armor, not to Walsh.

"I'm sorry for that." Walsh laid his hands on my shoulders. "But you can't let anyone see it. If Mrs. Hale is worried enough to start playing matchmaker, how long until she tries to talk to someone in the Ice Domes to find out more about you? Our computer files are ironclad, but there's no teacher for anyone to ask about Lanni Roberts."

"Shit." I dug my knuckles into my eyes. Somehow, my forehead ended up against Walsh's shoulder.

"You just have to date someone. Spend a couple weeks pretending to be happy, have a bad breakup, and then you can go back to silent and lonely while you mend your broken heart."

"So, just pick one of the guys and pretend to care about a kep?"

"Gideon would jump at the chance, but I would probably be your best bet."

I coughed out a laugh.

"I'm making you a genuine offer here." There wasn't a hint of teasing in Walsh's tone. "You'd have to, at the very least, spend some significant time kissing Gideon. You and I could just sneak into the trees and let people assume things."

"Is that what we're doing now?" I looked up at him. My face was close enough to his, if anyone found us, they would think we were about to kiss.

"This is just a safe place to talk, but we could play it off as more. Added bonus, you wouldn't have to lie to me about who you are. Pretending to be someone else is exhausting."

"And what would you get out of it?"

"Pretending is exhausting for me, too."

"I know less about you than you do about me."

Walsh leaned down, kissing my cheek before whispering in my ear. "But at least you won't press me for answers about why I transferred to the Arc Domes alone. Just think about it." He stepped away from me. "And don't take too long. Mrs. Hale is going to run out of guys to send you up here with. And if she gets desperate—"

"Then I risk all of us getting caught because I suck at adapting to life in a glass cage."

"Come on." Walsh offered me his elbow. "We've got to go meet Mr. Strand. I can't wait to hear all the wonderful things he's got to say about his contributions to the early days of the domes."

"The bench is sturdy." I took Walsh's arm. "Just grip it really hard when you want to scream."

"Thanks for the advice." Walsh led me back out of the trees and onto a well-manicured path. "Lanni, that was nice. To actually talk to someone."

"Yeah. I think—"

The blaring siren and flashing red lights drove what I was going to say from my mind.

A little girl by the pond started screaming.

The screaming and the sirens and the flashing lights, all of it seemed obscene against the atrium's façade of beautiful perfection.

"Why are the sirens going off?" Walsh shifted my grip from his elbow to his hand.

I didn't have an answer for him.

There were plenty of kep guards around, but none of them seemed to be attacking any of the people fleeing the atrium. There was no smoke. I hadn't felt an explosion. The only one screaming was the little girl.

"I need to get to Mari." I ran to join the fleeing crowd.

Walsh stayed beside me while we weaved through the kep running for the steps that led out of the atrium.

Two guards in black uniforms flanked the top of the staircase.

"What's going on?" A woman stood by one of the guards, her hands on her hips as she glared tiredly at the man, not seeming to care about the gun on his belt.

"No idea, ma'am," the guard said. "I only know all citizens are to report to the nearest bunker."

Bunker.

I'd vaguely known there were bunkers in the domes—there were arrows painted on the walls displaying directions to safety—but it hadn't occurred to me I'd ever see the inside of one.

"Where's Mari?" Walsh asked as we hurried down the stairs.

"I sent her over to our guardian's house. She lives at the back of Bloom Dome."

At the bottom of the steps, everyone turned left.

I started to run straight ahead, along the quickest route to Miranda's.

"Get to the bunker." A guard held out his hand, blocking my path.

"I have to get to Bloom Dome." I tried to step around him.

He grabbed my arm, holding me in place. "To the bunker. Now."

"My sister's there. She's only seven," I said. "I have to make sure she's safe."

"I will not ask you again." The guard shoved me back.

"Lanni, she'll be okay." Walsh gripped my hand.

I broke away from Walsh. I didn't register any pain in my hand as I swung and punched the guard in the jaw, but as I sprinted down the tunnel, I did hear the pop of his gun as he shot a silver dart into my neck.

CHAPTER EIGHT

They've damaged so many of us.

I know how widespread the Incorporation's evil is. I know they've claimed so many innocent lives there will never be a true tally of their victims. Somehow, it still never occurred to me that there would be people outside our cause who want to fight. I don't know if that makes me naïve or cynical. Either way, even if the other battle against the Incorporation won't aid our cause, the fact that another fight exists gives me hope.

A set of domes has fallen. Not one I'd ever seen, but somewhere in the world, someone dared to fight against the demons who hide behind glass, and they won.

I wonder how their battle ended. Did they move their army into the domes, or smash the glass so no new evil could grow from the apathy created by a life of ease?

In some childish way, I almost think knowing how their story ended would make my mission seem less futile.

I still don't know what end I'm fighting to reach. The only thing I'm sure of is that I will fight as long as there is breath in my body. There can be no other choice for me.

But if we do fail, if giving my body and my life for our cause isn't enough to buy us success, knowing that someone else far away defeated their domes gives me hope that, as long as the Incorporation survives, another rebellion will form. Another group will fight, and one day, even if it's years from now, the bastards will all burn.

We outnumber them. There are more of us than there are of the demons, and even if victory has to be bought in blood, there are enough of us willing to pay the cost of freedom. We can save the ones who will come long after we've fallen.

See you in the embers,

-C

CHAPTER NINE

The thumping in my head distracted me from the rubbery feeling inside my mouth. I focused on the pain in my skull, trying to figure out what could be crashing into my head over and over at such a steady rhythm. The pain came from the inside, like my brain was bashing against its cage, trying to escape the ache that filled my body like cement had taken the place of the blood in my veins.

I started to open my eyes, but the bright lights around me only made the thumping worse.

"Shh, you're okay." Someone shifted me, like they were trying to cradle me to their chest. "You have to wait it out, but you'll be okay."

"What happened?" The heaviness of my tongue slurred my words.

"You punched a guard, tried to bolt past, and took a dart to the neck." A laugh rumbled against my shoulder. "Not the best thing to happen, but since you were panicking about Mari, I think we can play it off."

I opened my eyes again, just enough to see the face of the person who held me.

Walsh smiled as he looked down at me. He had settled me in his lap, his arms wrapped around me to keep my head on his shoulder as I slept.

"Where's Mari?" I tried to push away from Walsh, but my arms were too heavy to move.

"I begged our door guard to radio around." Walsh shifted his arm, tipping my head so I could see him more easily. "Mari's in the bunker below seed storage with Miranda. She's safe."

"Thank you." My eyes started drifting closed. "Why are we here? Did we get attacked?"

"I couldn't get the guard to tell me anything about that. But he seemed pissed and a little scared."

"That's not good." I forced my eyes back open, but I couldn't get them to focus on anything farther away than Walsh's face.

"No, it's really not."

"We can't just sit here." I tried to move away from Walsh, but he held me so tight, I only managed to flop my head to the side. "The room's swoopy. Oh, that's awful."

My stomach rolled as the people around me wobbled like they were riding on the waves in the Salt Dome.

"I feel sick."

"You're okay." Walsh shifted me to sit more upright and rubbed slow circles on my back like I would've done with Mari. "Just breathe."

"You should put me on the floor." I took a deep breath that didn't actually make me feel any better.

"Getting puked on wouldn't be the worst thing to have happened to me this year."

I took another breath, and the swaying in the room slowed down enough I could actually focus on the people around me.

Long strips of benches ran along either side of the concrete room, with smaller benches running down the middle. Almost everyone had taken a seat on a bench, but a few people paced in the aisles. Two guards stood beside the only door in the space. There was no window, no visible hatch, no way out.

"They locked us in." I managed to lift my arm enough to push against Walsh's chest. "We have to get out. They locked us in."

"We're supposed to be locked in. This is a bunker."

"Would a bunker have helped at the depot?"

"No." Walsh brushed my hair away from my face before tilting my head sideways to rest on his shoulder. "But that's not going to happen here."

"How do you know?" My eyes started to sag again.

"Just trust me, Lanni. I won't let anything happen to you."

Before I could rearrange the sludge in my brain into words, I'd started drifting to sleep.

"I don't trust anybody."

I don't know if I actually managed to say the words as everything faded back to black.

CHAPTER TEN

"Not anybody." My mouth moved more easily as I formed the words, but something else felt off.

Dry grit filled my throat. I wasn't as warm as I had been. And I was lying down. Something soft kept my arms from moving.

"What is this?" I moved my hands. Fabric covered them.

"Actually awake this time?"

"Lanni!" Mari said right before something landed on my legs.

"Careful with her, kiddo. She's going to feel like shit."

I opened my eyes.

Red hair blocked out the overhead light.

"Harper?" I blinked up at her face.

"I'll take that as a *yes*." Harper lifted Mari off my legs. "Get her some water."

"Mari, are you okay?" I tried to sit up, but my arms shook too badly. "I tried to get to you."

"I was with Miranda. I was okay." Mari leaned down, draping her arms around me as she pressed her cheek to mine. "I'm sorry you got shot."

"I'm okay." I dragged my arms out from under the sheets to give Mari a proper hug.

I wasn't ready to let go when Mari wriggled away from me to go to the kitchen part of our room.

"How did I get here?" I asked.

"Walsh carried you. He wanted to stay, but I kicked him out." Harper shifted the pillows, helping me sit up. "It was the only way to make Guardian Miranda leave," she added in a whisper.

"What happened? Why did the alarms go off?" My arm ached as I took the water glass from Mari.

Harper tipped her head toward Mari.

"You can talk in front of me," Mari said. "You're not going to scare me."

"She'll be fine," I said.

"There was an explosion in the medical corridor." Harper dragged her hands over her short hair.

"How big an explosion?" I pushed myself away from my pillows, trying to think through where I should hide Mari if someone who wanted to hurt the kep had gotten inside the domes. I'd been panicking about what to do if the kep found out we didn't belong, or if monsters surged up the mountainside, but not how I'd protect her if violence began within the glass.

"I don't think it was too big," Harper said. "I swung by on my way back here. There's definitely some damage, but the ceiling in the medical corridor is still up."

I took a sip of water. Crisp and clean and everything the domes were supposed to be.

"Could it have been an accident?" I asked. "Or a mechanical issue? Did something malfunction?"

"Could be." Harper shrugged. "But we won't know anything until the Domes Council decides to tell us. Which from my experience should be just about...never."

"But if someone's trying to hurt us, we have to know." Mari crawled up onto the foot of my bed.

"Protecting us is the guards' job," Harper said.

"What if I don't trust the guards to do their job?" I said.

"Tough shit," Harper said. "That's how things work in the domes, and someone who's lived inside glass their whole life should be used to it."

"And people are just okay with it?" I fought to keep my anger out of my voice.

"Of course they are." Harper stood up. "We all must do our duty to the domes. And sometimes, that duty involves shutting up and moving on. Drink a few more glasses of water before you go to sleep, or you'll wake up with a hangover from hell in the morning."

"How do you know?" Mari asked.

"I lost a bet." Harper bopped Mari on the nose before heading for the door. "Scream real loud if you need me."

"Night, Harper," I called after her as she closed the door.

Harper really would've been able to hear it if Mari or I screamed. She lived at the front of our building, only three doors down and across the hall.

If I waited until Mari went to sleep, I could sneak over to Harper's and see if there was anything she didn't want to say in front of Mari. Or if I really was just supposed to shut up and hope our home hadn't been attacked.

Our home.

I hated myself for even thinking the words.

"You have to drink more." Mari crawled toward me, settling herself right by my side.

"Yes, doctor." I chugged the rest of the glass.

"Miranda was worried about you, too, you know." Mari rolled herself off the bed. "She made a fuss to the guards."

"That was nice of her."

"Miranda was going to go through my homework with me." Mari filled my glass and brought it back to me.

"Did you need help with it?" I sipped the second round of water.

"No. But it sounded like fun." Mari chewed her lips together.

"She said I could go to her house tomorrow since we didn't get to finish tonight. If it's okay with you."

"Sure. If that's what you want to do."

A smile lit Mari's face. "She said she'd braid my hair fancy, too."

I was saved from having to worry about the odd feeling in my stomach that hovered somewhere between self-loathing and left-over nausea by a ding from PAM.

Schedule Adjustment

Report to the Domes Council's chamber at 8:00 a.m. tomorrow.

CHAPTER ELEVEN

My hands wouldn't stop sweating as I waited outside the Domes Council's chamber.

I wished I could have been in some far away corridor where I could pace and panic in peace, but the chamber was up near the atrium where I could almost see the place I'd bolted past the guards.

I couldn't bring myself to feel guilty for trying to get to Mari. She was my sister. She was mine to protect. Not Miranda's, and certainly not some kep guard's.

But I had to pretend to feel sorry for it. Had to act like a traumatized girl. Had to hope punching a guard wasn't a big enough offense to get me kicked out of the domes or have the Council start asking questions about the three orphans transferred from the Ice Domes.

When I'd woken Harper up after Mari went to bed, she'd told me to just cry and say how sorry I was.

What if I wasn't a good enough liar to convince the Council I was sorry?

I wiped my palms off on my pants.

A woman with two little kids in tow passed me on her way to

the atrium. None of them looked at me like I was about to be executed. That was good.

I should have stayed with Mari longer. Or gone up to the atrium to walk around before my meeting. Or brought my tablet so I could do schoolwork.

"Miss Roberts." A familiar voice spoke from behind me.

I turned toward the door to the Council chamber.

Alec's name was halfway to my lips before I noticed the rigid set of his mouth.

He didn't look like himself.

Since we'd arrived at the Arc Domes, I'd seen him in passing and talked to him a few times. He'd always smile like he was happy to see me, then furrow his brow when he asked how I was doing, like he genuinely understood that life hadn't become perfect even though we'd managed to lock Mari and me inside the glass.

Now, he just looked worried and tense. I didn't know if the warning in his eyes meant the Council had just reprimanded him or if he was trying to tell me I was about to walk into hell.

"Guard Quinn." I kept my voice soft in case even that acknowledgement was too much.

He gave me a nod so small I couldn't be sure if it had really happened or if I was just so desperate for comfort I'd imagined it.

"They're ready for you." Alec opened the door to the room for me.

I didn't let myself hesitate before stepping inside. Maybe I should have hesitated. Maybe that's what a vulnerable young woman would do.

A table with six people all facing toward the door waited for me. A single chair sat in front of them, like they'd prepared the space just for me.

I glanced back as the door closed behind me. Alec hadn't come into the room with me.

"Miss Roberts," the woman who sat in one of the two center-most seats said.

"Yes, ma'am." I took a step closer to the table, pressing my hands to the sides of my legs to resist reaching for the knife I knew I didn't have.

"Take a seat." The woman pointed to the lone chair.

"Yes, ma'am."

The whole Council watched me as I walked to the chair. I didn't know what they were looking for, what part I was supposed to play.

If you don't know what to say, just cry, Harper's voice whispered in my mind.

I scooted the chair forward an inch as I sat, not because I wanted to sit closer to the Council, just to make sure it was a normal chair and not some evil kep invention that could trap and torture me.

"Miss Roberts," the woman said, "do you know why we called you in this morning?"

"Yes, ma'am."

The woman waited for a moment before speaking again. "And why would that be?"

"I punched a guard and tried to run past him while the sirens were going off, ma'am." I laid my hands in my lap.

"And why would you choose to do such a foolish thing?" the woman said.

"I didn't choose to, ma'am. It just happened."

"I think what Mrs. Adair means is, what led to it happening?" The man next to Mrs. Adair rested his clasped hands on the table. He wore a black guard's uniform. The black badge on his chest meant he was an Outer Guard, one of the elite tasked with protecting the kep from all threats beyond the glass walls. The name *Captain Pace* on his badge meant I was right to feel like bolting from the room might actually be my safest option.

"I'd been in the atrium for a school assignment, sir." I forced my voice to stay steady. "The sirens went off, and I didn't know where my little sister was. I was on my way back to Bloom Dome, the guard told me to stop, and I just couldn't. I had to get back to Mari. I had to make sure she was safe."

"And once you were past the guard?" Captain Pace asked.

"I don't remember much," I said. "I heard a pop, and everything went dark. I came to a bit in the bunker, but not all the way until I got home."

"And was your sister there?" Mrs. Adair asked.

"Yes, ma'am," I said. "Thankfully, she'd been with our guardian, Miranda. She took Mari to the bunker on the other side of the domes with her."

"And what did we learn from this?" Mrs. Adair asked.

To never leave Mari alone.

"I'm not sure, ma'am." I bit my lips together, trying to riddle through what a good citizen of the domes would say.

"You're not sure?" Mrs. Adair leaned toward me.

"To listen to the guards." I met Mrs. Adair's gaze.

"And?" she prompted.

"That we should give the girl some latitude," Captain Pace said. "She survived the attack at the depot. After living through that sort of trauma, not being able to suppress the instinct to defend when threatened by an unknown danger—"

"There was no danger," Mrs. Adair cut across.

"How was she to know that?" a woman at the end of the table in a white doctor's uniform said.

"She survived an attack that killed more than a hundred Incorporation citizens," Captain Pace said. "Even a trained guard would have lasting reactionary damage. She bruised one man's jaw. The girl lost a bit of sense when she was trying to help the sister that has been entrusted to her care."

"Thank you, sir," I said.

"And what should we do about it?" Mrs. Adair folded her hands in front of her. "Even if we can agree she meant no harm and forgive her lapse in judgment, we can't risk this behavior occurring again."

"Do the sirens go off often?" The question came out meeker than I knew I was capable of sounding, like I was a girl who could actually be frightened by flashing lights and loud noises. I dug my nails into my thighs.

"No." Captain Pace gave me a kind smile that made me question how he'd been chosen as the leader of the Arc Domes' Outer Guard.

"Then why did the sirens go off?" I asked. "Sir."

"That's not for you to worry about," Mrs. Adair said. "You need to trust the guards when they give you directions, and you need to trust this Council to maintain the safety of the Arcadia Domes."

"Yes, ma'am."

"Maintenance can always use an extra set of hands," a man with slicked back, white hair said. "With the extra work they now have, I'm sure they'd be grateful."

"I'd like her to start in the new program," Captain Pace said.

The others at the table all turned toward him.

"We are actively discouraging female enlistment," Mrs. Adair said.

"Who says she has to enlist?" Captain Pace said. "She's seen fighting. She's seen the consequences. That caravan was protected by a full complement of guards, and the depot still got blown to hell. I can't blame her for doubting our ability to protect her sister. Let her see how the guards work and train her to defend herself. Knowing how to fight can be a comforting thing, and she'll learn to follow orders, which is this Council's aim."

The Council looked from Captain Pace to me.

"You'll take responsibility for her recommitment to our rules?" Mrs. Adair said.

"I would be happy to," Captain Pace said.

"Excellent," Mrs. Adair said. "We're done here. PAM will notify you of your new schedule."

"Thank you, ma'am." I glanced back over my shoulder, hoping to see Alec opening the door.

"You may go, Miss Roberts. Send in our next appointment."

"Yes, ma'am." I stood and walked as calmly as I could, not really breathing until I'd slipped into the hall.

A middle-aged man waited in the corridor.

"I think they're ready for you," I said.

"Perfect." The man sighed before walking into the Council chamber.

I stood in the hall, staring at the concrete walls for a long moment, not sure if everything was going to be all right or not.

"Haven't been kicked out of the domes," I whispered to myself as I started toward Bloom Dome to get my tablet. "No words like *traitor*. That's nice."

I turned to go down the stairs to the level of tunnels that led to most of the domes.

"Lanni." Alec waited beside the stairs, his hands tucked behind his back like he was on guard duty.

"Are you hauling me to another meeting? I'm already late for class."

"Just wanted to check in with you. See how you've been doing." There was something in the set of his face that made the tension I'd just been able to release from between my shoulder blades double.

"Can we walk?" I nodded toward the stairs. "I left my tablet at home. I wasn't sure if I was going to be flogged, and I didn't want to risk the screen getting cracked."

Alec laughed like I'd been joking.

I gave a little chuckle to play along.

"How did it go?" His tone softened, like he'd decided it was safe to be Alec instead of Guard Quinn.

"With Mrs. Adair and the squad of doom? Fine, I think. I'm

supposed to start in some new program. I'm not sure what it is, but I guess I'll learn to follow orders and defend myself."

Alec stopped halfway down the stairs. "You're joining Captain Pace's program?"

"Yes? They weren't really too clear on the details."

Alec dragged his hands over his hair.

"Is that a problem?"

He started down the steps again. "Could be worse."

"Are you going to be stingy with the details, too?"

We both stayed silent as a couple walked past.

"It's a training program for people who are still in school," Alec said. "It prepares students to enlist as Outer Guard."

"What?" It was my turn to stop walking.

Alec took my arm, guiding me forward as a group of maintenance workers walked past, heading toward the damage in the medical corridor.

"It won't be that bad. You'll learn basic combat techniques," Alec said, "some physical drills, things like that. These domes have lost a lot of guards recently."

"From the depot?"

"There and the River Domes." Alec glanced toward me. "You were right. The River Domes really did fall in an attack. The Incorporation had sent a large number of guards from the Arcadia Domes to help defend the River Domes. All of them died. So did the head of all the Incorporation's guards."

"Is that why the kep attacked the vampires back home?" I pulled my arm from his grip. "Alec?"

"I don't know. The higher-ups rarely share the *why* with the Outer Guard. We're just supposed to do as we're told."

"And kill people?"

"And hope it doesn't come to that, but there are never any guarantees," Alec said. "The guards who were sent to the River Domes were supposed to come back. The Arc Domes are desperately short on Outer Guard. They're going to need a bigger batch from the next few sets of students to fill out their ranks. The training program is meant to accelerate that process."

"I can't be an Outer Guard. I can't go out there and fight people who are just trying to survive." I grabbed his arm to make him stop walking. "It would—" A shiver of revulsion stole my voice. "It would be like attacking myself. My family—"

"I know." Alec lifted my hand from his arm, holding it in his. "You won't have to join the guards. We'll figure it out."

"Are you sure?" I gripped his hand tighter, focusing on the feel of his skin against mine, fighting to find an anchor strong enough to keep me from falling into a spiral of panic and self-loathing.

"Absolutely. Just do me a favor, and don't be too good in training. It'll make things easier." His smile didn't reach his eyes. "About last night...are you okay?" He said it like he was testing my balance.

"I'd be better if I knew what had happened."

"You're not supposed to know that."

"Because knowing that would be the biggest problem the Incorporation could have with me?" I whispered.

That smile did reach his eyes. His swallowed laughter glinted in their emerald-green.

He kept my hand in his as he started down the hall again, like he understood how much I needed that simple touch and didn't think finding comfort in his palm pressing against mine made me awful or weak.

We climbed the stairs to Bloom Dome.

I started toward the path that went to my building. But Alec led me the other way, onto a side path that cut between lilac trees. He looked around, scanning all the shadows before speaking.

"There was an explosion in medical storage."

"What kind of explosion? A bad chemical reaction? A bomb?"

"I don't know the details, but from the sounds of it, the device was well-made and deliberately planted."

I looked through the trees toward my building. It was solidly built, but not strong enough to withstand a bomb. "Was it the people who attacked the depot? If they've found a way in, I have to get Mari out. I can't keep her here."

Alec touched my chin, tipping my face up so I would meet his gaze. "There's no proof of that."

"There's no proof of the Incorporation doing anything to even try and figure out who attacked the depot. What if the same people followed us here? What if the kep don't bother investigating this bombing either?"

"There's a whole team of Outer Guard investigating what happened at the depot, and a team of Dome Guard will be assigned to investigate what happened last night. The Incorporation likes to keep things quiet, but they haven't forgotten that our caravan was attacked. They'll figure out who it was, and we'll be safe again."

"I'm starting to think safety is a lie."

"You and Mari are going to be okay." He laid his hands on my shoulders. I missed the warmth of his hand holding mine. "I made a promise to keep you safe. I'm going to keep my end of the deal."

"What deal?"

"With Amery." Alec lifted his hands away, tucking them behind his back, diving back into being Guard Quinn. "If you ever want to hear about him, I'll tell you about the deal."

"Why not now?"

"It's not a simple story. It wouldn't make sense without understanding Amery, and I can't...it's not something I can rush through explaining. I have to make sure I get all the pieces in the right place. You should get to class." He gave me a nod and walked away, like mentioning the father who'd decided to save me by ripping me away from my life was as normal as the explosion in medical storage.

"Why would anyone want to blow up medical storage?" I tried to reason through it as I ran to my building to grab my tablet.

I spent the walk to class coming up with a list of better targets for an attack.

Taking out the guards' weapons storage would be my top choice, though admittedly I'd never actually gotten to see that part of the domes since access was restricted. Normal kep weren't allowed anywhere near the bay where the domes' vehicles were kept, either. I knew there was a massive storage system beneath the lowest of the tiered domes, but only workers needing access were allowed down that far.

Normal kep could get to food storage. I'd been in the water purification rooms for class, too. I couldn't come up with a logical explanation for why anyone would leave the kep's food and water but ruin their medical supplies.

They must not understand how terrible a death dehydration and starvation offer.

I stopped outside my classroom as my stomach rolled and sour shot into my throat.

I couldn't remember what I'd eaten for breakfast. Mari had shoved a bunch of food at me and demanded I finish it all or she wouldn't eat.

I'd just shoveled everything down. I couldn't remember how many glasses of water I'd had, either.

I leaned against the wall, pressing my forehead to the concrete. The ache in my skull didn't make my stomach feel any better.

"Lanni." Mrs. Hale popped her head out of the classroom door. "Are you feeling all right?"

"Fine." I pressed a smile onto my face. "Just couldn't sleep after the excitement yesterday."

"I don't blame you. Do you feel up to joining class?"

"Yes, ma'am." I pushed away from the wall. "A distraction would be great."

"Wonderful. I hope that means you're up to meeting Mr.

Strand tonight. He was so disappointed when everything had to be cancelled."

"Sounds great." I followed Mrs. Hale into the classroom where a picture of a strand of DNA took up the entire wall.

The whole class looked at me instead of at the image as I took my seat.

"I'll swing by to get you tonight?" Walsh asked loudly enough for the whole class to hear.

"Sure," I said. "Just no alarms this time."

"Don't worry, I can carry you home." Walsh winked at me, and wave of laughter, from giggles to snorts, swept around the class.

I even managed to laugh a little as I rolled my eyes at him.

Mrs. Hale grinned as she restarted the lesson.

Gideon looked over his shoulder, glancing between Walsh and me before whispering, "I'm really glad you're okay, Lanni. You had me worried."

"Thanks."

Mrs. Hale beamed as she swept the DNA picture away and moved on to an image of a many-limbed family tree.

CHAPTER TWELVE

Trust. That's the first thing joining our ranks demands. Before you can even begin to wonder if the changes are worth it, you have to trust the changes are possible.

Then, you have to trust that a needle to the heart will do more than just kill you, and that the person you'll be on the other side will be close enough to who you were that you'll still believe in our mission.

You have to trust the one who injects you, and the one who sits by your side as the drug blazes through your veins, like the dose is burning away everything you are. You have to trust them when they shout over your screams of pain, promising the fire in your blood will never die completely, but your body will adapt to the flames.

You trust the one who teaches you to fight. You trust the one who gives you to your captain.

You trust the men and women who fight by your side, and when your captain sends you into battle, you don't question. You just go.

That's the way things are supposed to work.

From the moment I learned our kind existed and what they'd set out to do, I knew I wanted to join. Even as I've doubted my humanity and what the future might look like if we succeed, I've never once questioned the loyalty of my brethren.

I came into this place willing to die. I know my mission may demand my life.

But what if they're willing to sacrifice me for an end I don't even know about?

If it's one of my pack that's made my task so much more dangerous, then I've undoubtedly been betrayed.

The spark might not have been made by one of our kind. There could be another monster hunting the Incorporation.

But I'm not sure.

I'm not sure I can trust the people who sent me here.

The doubting makes the blood in my veins burn hotter. I may turn to ash before my work is even finished.

See you in the embers,

-C

I walked Mari to Miranda's that night. If I could have skipped out on the assignment and stayed with Mari, I would have. But I couldn't risk causing a fuss.

Someone had attacked the domes, whether or not the guards wanted to admit it. Someone had set off a bomb, and the kep had no idea who'd done it.

I waited outside my building for Walsh and silently followed him toward the atrium. He chatted, and I tried to nod and laugh to fill all the right pauses. But I couldn't really hear what he was saying. I was too busy searching the halls for devices that might blow me apart.

We passed a few guards in the corridors, but not nearly enough to protect a place under attack.

I never thought I'd see the day when I'd want more kep guards around, but I did. I wanted them in full riot gear, lining the halls and trying to find the person who'd planted the bomb.

"You okay?" Walsh nudged me with his elbow.

"Yeah, why?" I picked up our pace as we climbed the stairs to the atrium.

"You stopped pretending to laugh at my jokes."

"Can we go back to the trees? I want to look at something."

"Sure." A tiny wrinkle in Walsh's brow gave the only hint that he knew I had no interest in the stream. He had bags under his eyes, like he hadn't been able to sleep after the bunker, either.

Both of us stayed silent until we'd reached the place where the water bubbled over the rocks. Walsh held up a finger to keep me silent as he listened for a moment.

"Are you sure they don't have cameras watching in the trees?" I asked.

"Yes, but only ask things like that once you're sure there are no lovebirds mating in the shadows."

"This isn't a joke."

"Setting fornication aside, why would you need to know where it's safe to talk?" Walsh tucked his hands into his pockets.

I stepped close enough to him to be able to whisper. "Someone planted a bomb in medical storage. The explosion was deliberate. I don't know why or who, but blowing things up is a pretty clear attack against the Arc Domes."

I waited for Walsh to say something, but he just stared down at the water.

"If whoever attacked the depot is behind this, we're all in massive trouble," I said.

"You mean the Incorporation is." Walsh finally looked back up at me.

"No. You, me, Mari—we're fucked, too. The three of us almost died when the depot was attacked. Bombs don't care how you got into the domes database. They just kill everyone within the blast radius."

"What kind of device was it? What was the target?"

"No idea. And I hate that I'm relieved you don't know either. Two months ago, I wouldn't have cared who wanted to blow up the kep. If people are strong enough to fight the Incorporation, they should. Murderers in glass palaces shouldn't be ruling the world."

"But now you and Mari are in here." Walsh rocked back on his heels.

"I have to keep her safe, and I don't know how to do that." A knot pressed on the front of my throat. "Walsh, I don't know what to do."

He started to reach for me before tucking his hands back into his pockets. "Will you trust me?"

"I don't know if I'm capable of trusting anybody anymore."

He furrowed his brow. Beads of sweat shone on his forehead.

"I don't blame you," Walsh said. "But we're both outsiders. We're fighting for the same thing."

"The only thing I'm fighting for is keeping Mari safe."

"I promise you, we're on the same side. I just need you to do one thing for me."

"If it's keep my head down, I'll punch you."

"Don't look too closely, and if shit hits the fan, find Demetrius." He walked away, heading toward the glass.

"What the fuck is that supposed to mean?" I chased after him.

"That's all I can give you, Lanni." Sweat had started to bead on the back of his neck.

"Walsh, are you okay?"

He flinched when I touched his arm.

"Just nervous about meeting a legend like Mr. Strand, I guess."

We stepped off a path that had somehow led us around to the bench under the red-leafed trees where I'd met with the rest of the elders for my evening assignments.

He was watching me.

For a moment, I wanted to punch him in the back of the head, but if he could follow me around the domes, maybe he really could help me take care of Mari. And I wouldn't have to lie to him about why I needed the help.

"Why is Strand a legend?" I asked.

"You didn't do your research before coming to meet me?"

I turned toward the voice.

The man was as old as the others I'd met, but age hadn't withered him.

His back was straight and his stride long as he took the last few steps toward us. He looked from me to Walsh, and there was something in his gaze that made it seem like he was thinking about the fastest way to kill me.

"Mr. Strand, sir, it's an honor." Walsh stepped forward, giving Mr. Strand a nod before shaking his hand.

I fought to make myself smile as I reached for Strand's hand.

"Lanni, Mr. Strand was one of the original team members." Walsh cut between Strand and me, saving me from having to touch the kep and herding me toward the bench. "He was the first head of the Arcadia Domes' Outer Guard and spent years developing some of the domes' most efficient weapons."

"That's impressive." I sat, gripping the edge of the bench to keep my hands from shaking as I fought the urge to strangle Mr. Strand.

"You'll have to forgive Lanni." Walsh sat beside me. "She took a dart to the neck yesterday and is still feeling a bit woozy."

"For someone of your size, the full effects should be out of your system in twenty-eight hours." Strand sat on the bench opposite us. "Took nearly six months to create a formula strong enough to take down a large man but mild enough not to kill a child."

"Lucky for Lanni you were so"—Walsh swallowed before continuing—"careful in your testing."

I glanced at Walsh, trying to see if he wanted to strangle Strand as badly as I did. But he just tipped his chin down and blinked, almost like he was trying to stop the trees around us from spinning.

"Those were the good days," Strand said. "Testing, experiments, inventing. It takes a lot to be a good guard, more to lead the guards, but inventing the tools that will protect the domes...

that's where I've truly left my mark. And the work doesn't end when your body starts to slow down."

"How do you mean?" I reached for Walsh's hand.

He flinched and pulled away from me, shoving his hands into his pockets.

"The rest who remain from the original team have all retired. They spend their days puttering. They value their time to relax, a reward for all the work they've done. But purpose is what keeps a man alive." Strand tapped his knuckles over his heart. "If you don't have something to wake up for every morning, the body and mind start to decay."

I glanced to Walsh, waiting for him to say something. But he'd clenched his jaw like he was convincing himself not to make a sound. Beads of sweat ran down the sides of his neck.

"I hadn't heard that before," I said. "But it makes sense. If you don't have something to work toward, you'll stop. Then your body will stop, too."

"I greet the sunrise every morning." Strand stood and paced between the benches. "I spend my days in the lab, working for the good of the Incorporation. To be completely frank, I should be in my lab working right now, but it's my duty to pass my knowledge on to future generations."

"If you don't have time to talk to us, I completely understand." I reached out to touch Walsh's arm. Even through his shirt, his skin felt too hot. "Actually, I'm starting to feel nauseous from the sedative in the dart again. I'd be so embarrassed if I got sick in front of you. Maybe Walsh should walk me home before I start throwing up."

"If you're feeling ill, best to let it out," Strand said. "Can't let toxins dwell in the body."

The rhythm of Strand's footsteps faltered.

"I'll let it out as soon as Walsh gets me home." I grabbed Walsh's arm, yanking him to his feet. He swayed and stumbled forward a step. "Do you need a doctor?"

"We have to stay." Walsh spoke through gritted teeth.

"I thought you were the one..." Strand's words faded away. His chest started twitching. He made an awful gagging noise like he was gulping for air but couldn't get a breath.

"Mr. Strand, are you all right?" I let go of Walsh and moved toward Strand.

"Lanni, don't."

There was something in the way Walsh said it that made me leap back, both hands held in front of my chest as though I needed to prove I hadn't touched Strand.

Strand took one step toward me before his knees buckled and he crashed to the ground. He stared into my eyes as the convulsing of his chest got smaller and faster.

"Don't scream," Walsh whispered.

Strand's arms and legs started to shake, bouncing on the moss-covered ground as his eyes rolled back in his head. He made a sound like he was choking on something, and then he went still.

I froze for a heartbeat, then another, waiting for something to happen.

"What the fuck was that?" My voice shook.

"Just stay quiet." Walsh fell to his knees beside the stream.

"What's wrong with you?" I knelt next to him.

"I'll be fine. Just give me a minute." He dipped his hands into the stream, scrubbing them together before pulling a pill-sized capsule from his pocket. He dipped the capsule into the stream, and it started to foam like soap. He scrubbed his hands with the foam and wiped some on Strand's palm. He used his shirt to wipe the foam back off Strand's skin before dipping his own hands into the water again.

"What the hell is going on?" I asked.

Walsh splashed water on his face and neck. "How calm are you?"

"Really fucking calm considering I'm pretty sure Strand is dead."

"He is." Walsh took a breath and pushed himself to his feet.

I caught his elbow as he swayed.

"I need you to scream for help," Walsh said.

"What?" I glanced through the trees, convinced black-uniformed guards were going to charge out to kill us at any moment.

"Scream for help. Strand fell, convulsed, and went still. It was over in less than ten seconds."

"Why shouldn't I tell them what actually happened?" I let go of Walsh's arm.

"Because if they find out I killed him, they'll start investigating how I got inside the domes."

CHAPTER FOURTEEN

"Help!" My scream wasn't loud enough. Wasn't panicked enough. "Help! I need help! Please!"

I knelt beside Strand, trying to think through what a kep would do. I reached toward him.

"Don't touch his hand," Walsh whispered as voices and footsteps came toward us. "Just in case."

"What's going on back here?" someone called.

I ignored the question.

"Mr. Strand?" I shook his shoulder. "Mr. Strand, wake up! Mr. Strand?"

"I don't think he has a pulse." Walsh pressed on Strand's wrist. *Of course he doesn't. You killed him.*

I shot Walsh a glare and patted Mr. Strand on the cheek. "Mr. Strand? I don't think he's breathing."

"Good god." Someone grabbed me under the arms, lifting me away from Strand like I was a little kid creeping too close to danger. "We're going to need medical."

I stumbled toward the bench. I gripped the back to steady myself, leaning over and staring wide-eyed at the growing chaos of the scene.

Two guards knelt beside Strand. One of them had pulled open the top of Strand's shirt while the other spoke into his own wrist.

More kep had gathered under the red trees, watching the scene like a corpse was a rare and morbid form of entertainment instead of the inevitable fate we would all someday meet.

"Everyone, move back," one of the guards ordered. "Clear the way for medical."

The crowd shifted deeper into the fake forest.

Walsh sank to the ground, leaning against a tree behind the bench.

I stumbled over and sat beside him, hoping that wasn't too logical a choice for someone who was supposed to be in shock.

"Medical coming through." Two doctors in white uniforms raced into view. "What happened?"

"It was so fast." Walsh's words came out airy and gritty, like he couldn't catch his breath.

"He didn't look sick," I said. "But he collapsed and he started twitching. I didn't know what was happening. It couldn't have been more than ten seconds before he went still. It was all over before I could even think to call for help."

"He doesn't have a pulse." One of the doctors opened her medical kit.

A man with a gurney arrived as the doctors stuck little gray pads to Strand's chest.

I pressed my palms to the ground, trying to convince myself there was no way Strand could wake up and tell everyone I'd lied.

Walsh leaned his head back against the tree. He took slow breaths, like he was fighting to make his lungs fill.

"Are you okay?" I twisted to kneel beside him.

"I just need a little more time."

I pressed my fingers to the side of his sweat-slicked neck. His skin burned against mine, too hot for a person to survive.

"You need help." I looked toward the doctors. They were still trying to revive Strand even as they loaded him onto a gurney.

"Don't." Walsh put a hand on my back. The heat of his palm carried through my shirt. "They're the last thing I need."

I leaned close to him, letting him wrap his arm around my waist as I whispered, "You owe me one hell of an explanation."

"I carry you around while your tranqed, and this is the thanks I get?" Walsh leaned his forehead against my shoulder. His breath rattled in his lungs.

The two guards watched the doctors take Strand away before looking to us.

"You're okay." I wrapped my arms around Walsh. "Just stay quiet and you'll be okay."

The guards studied the spot where Strand had fallen before coming to loom over us.

"Can you tell us more about what happened?" one of the guards said.

I tightened the front of my throat and bit my lips together before talking. "We were—we were sent here to meet Mr. Strand for a school assignment. He was telling us about the domes. How they were built and—and I think he seemed normal. I mean, we'd never met him before. And then he fell, and he was shaking, and then I called for help." I gave a little cough like I was holding back tears. "I couldn't do anything. I should—should've been able to do something."

"You're okay, Lanni. There's nothing we could have done. There just wasn't time." Walsh held me close while my shoulders shook with what I hoped looked like tears.

"We'll get your names," one of the guards said. "Are you two okay to head home by yourselves?"

"I'll get her home," Walsh said.

I tightened my grip on him, keeping my dry face hidden as he gave the guards our names. I didn't look up until their footsteps had faded.

I let go of Walsh, pulling away just enough to search the

shadows around us before speaking. "You'll get me home? Can you even stand?"

"Sure." Walsh winced as he dropped his arms from around my waist, like even that little movement had taken too much energy to bear. "I feel much better already."

"Better from what?" I stood and reached down for Walsh's hand.

"Not yet." Walsh planted his palms on the ground and pushed himself to his feet. "It's not safe. Not until I've washed them again. I need to make sure they're clean."

I wrapped my arm around his waist. "At least put your arm around my shoulders. You look like you're going to tip over."

"I might." Walsh draped his arm over my shoulders, and I pulled myself close to his side, hoping it would look more like I'd nestled near him for comfort than like I was worried about him making it to the stairs, let alone all the way home.

"Where do you live?" I asked.

"I'm in the Marsh Dome. I'm insulted you don't know." Walsh managed to keep his feet under himself as we headed toward the stairs.

"You're the one who's been lurking in the shadows watching me. I have a little sister to take care of. I don't have time to stalk anyone."

We cut around a pack of people who had all clustered together to gossip in hushed tones. Maybe they thought sounding shocked absolved them of any guilt they should have felt for making entertainment out of death. The rustle of their chatter followed us all the way to the stairwell.

I'm going to end up in front of the Council again for this.

"You're wrong." Walsh spoke through gritted teeth, keeping his pace steady even though he winced every time we went down a step.

"I do have time to stalk you? Should I bring Mari along and call it family fun?"

"I never stalked you." Walsh stopped and looked at me. "I was never watching you. I was watching the people around you. Making sure none of them hurt you. It might not seem like a big difference, but trust me, it matters."

"It's still creepy. And wrong."

"I figured you'd have bigger problems with me." He started down the steps again, his gait a little more even, like the movement caused him less pain.

"Oh, I do. I'm just going to wait until I can get a decent answer."

"I hope I don't disappoint."

News of Strand's death hadn't made it down into the tunnels yet. Everyone meandering through the corridors seemed normal. No panic. No gossip.

We passed a few of our classmates. Walsh took some of his weight off my shoulders as he gave them a smile and a wave. They nodded back at us.

"I think you might be stuck dating me for a while," Walsh said. "Between the bunker and us walking through the halls with our arms around each other—"

"I'm trying to make sure you don't fall over."

"I'll be fine." He grimaced, shifting so his arm really did just drape around me. "See? I can walk all on my own. You don't have to keep holding onto me if you don't want to."

"First of all, you're still burning up, and I'm not convinced you won't drop any second. I'll have a lot more luck keeping you on your feet than I will trying to haul you back off the floor. Second, I'm not letting you slip away until you tell me exactly what happened."

"So we're officially going steady? Don't worry, I'll be a perfect gentleman."

"Save your breath. I'm not one for fake flirting."

I'd gone into the Marsh Dome before, but somehow I'd forgotten the salty smell that wafted down the steps into the corridor. The air felt different too, like it thickened as we climbed the stairs into the dome.

It was Walsh's turn to keep me moving as we reached the top of the steps.

Channels of water cut through the high grass that rustled in the breeze from unseen vents. Footbridges led from one island of solid ground to another, providing the pathways between housing units. The buildings themselves were made of pale brown material, and the roofs had been covered with low grasses and flowers, letting them blend into the landscape.

A beautiful and calming little slice of the world preserved within the glass.

I hated it.

I looked down as we cut over the first footbridge. Fish swam in the crystal-clear canal. The water wasn't that deep, only up to my shoulders. If I hadn't needed answers from a half-dead asshole, I would have been tempted to jump into the canal and let the current wash away any trace that I'd ever been in the atrium.

We crossed five bridges before reaching Walsh's home. There weren't flowerbeds around the building, and the color was different, but other than that, it was the same as mine. One front door, then six doors lining the hall inside.

We stopped in front of the second door on the right.

"Can you open it?" Walsh pulled his arm off me and leaned against the wall.

I turned the knob and held the door open for him.

"Home sweet home." He went straight to the sink, turned on the faucet, and started scrubbing his hands.

I closed the door behind me. "You touched my shirt. Should I burn it? Was whatever you used on Strand on your hands?"

"You're quick, aren't you?" Walsh rinsed his hands and started scrubbing them again. "Go to my closet. Take one of my shirts. Practically speaking, you should be fine. The transfer rate from fabric to skin is minimal. But Mari's short enough, it could transfer to her face if she hugs you. We can't take that kind of risk."

"You're right, we can't. We can't do anything that puts Mari at risk. So what the hell were you thinking?"

"Just change your shirt." Walsh scrubbed his hands for a third time.

I pinched the inside-bottom of my shirt, carefully pulling it up over my head without letting the outside fabric touch me. I balled my shirt up and tossed it on the floor next to his bed. "And what is it that's on my shirt?"

Walsh dried his hands and pulled off his own shirt. Sweat clung to the muscles of his torso. He had a pale birthmark on the left side of his chest, but no scars that I could see. Whoever had sent him into the domes had done a good job of removing any traces of his life before I'd met him at the depot. "Do you really want to know?"

"Yes." Heat flooded my cheeks as I grabbed the first shirt I could find out of his closet.

"Dermal contact poison."

"What?"

"Poison that works with skin contact."

"And you put it on your hand?" I yanked on the clean shirt.

"Yeah, I did."

"Why the fuck would you do that?" I whisper-shouted at him.

"I didn't get sent here for fun, Lanni." Walsh pulled off his pants.

I fixed my gaze on the ceiling.

"I have a job to do," Walsh said. "I couldn't risk losing my shot with Strand for a second time, so a direct transfer from my hand to his was the best bet I had."

Everything in my chest went cold, like the world had started spinning too fast and my heart and lungs had slowed down, trying to give me time to make sense of the madness.

"Someone snuck you in here to kill Strand?" I sank down onto Walsh's bed, not caring about his nakedness anymore.

"Partially, yes." Walsh took fresh clothes from his closet.

"And the other part?"

"Sorry, can't tell you." Walsh looked to me, and something in his eyes almost made me believe he truly was sorry he couldn't tell me his whole story.

"You're an assassin."

"Not really." Walsh tugged his pants on.

"You just poisoned someone. That makes you an assassin." I dragged my hands over my face. I looked at my palms. "How the hell are you not dead right now? Strand was gone in what, a minute? Less? You were sweating and looked sick before we even met Strand. You should be dead."

"I'm a quick healer." Walsh pulled on his shirt and walked back to his kitchen. He didn't lean on the wall to stay steady. His hands didn't shake as he pulled down a glass and filled it with water.

"Regular people don't just heal from poison."

"I'm fine. Isn't that what matters?" Walsh handed me the glass.

"No, it's not. You just murdered someone, and I covered for you. I think I have a right to know what kind of freaky poison killed him but not you."

"It wasn't the poison." Walsh filled a glass for himself and leaned against the counter. "That was normal. I'm the freak."

I sipped my water. "Go on."

He downed his entire glass of water, looked at me, then turned back to the sink to refill his glass. "I'm not supposed to tell you."

"I'm not supposed to be a party to murder, but here we are."

"Is killing a man who should be on trial for crimes against humanity really murder?"

"Do not try to distract me." My legs shook as I stood and took the two steps to stand in front of Walsh. "You owe me an explanation, so talk."

Walsh stared into my eyes as he sipped his water. "Have you ever met a vampire? Seen how they heal?"

"I've worked for a vampire and known enough to be really sure you don't qualify. I've seen you eat food. I've seen you outside during the day. You didn't sun burn. I'm not an idiot. Don't try to play me."

"You're right. I'm not a vampire." Walsh set down his glass and pulled a knife from his kitchen drawer.

I watched him lift the blade. I'd just seen him kill a man, but for some reason, I had no instinct to run.

Walsh held his palm out to me before dragging the knife across his hand.

Normal, red blood spilled from the wound, but as I watched, his skin knit back together like the blade had never cut him at all.

CHAPTER FIFTEEN

"What are you?" I grabbed Walsh's wrist, moving his hand over the sink before his blood could fall onto the floor.

I turned on the water, and the blood washed away, leaving his palm perfect.

"You're not a vampire." I grabbed the towel and dried his hand. "You're certainly not a regular human."

"Does it really matter?"

"Yes." I ran my finger along where the cut should have been. There wasn't even a ridge in its place.

"The drug that changed me is a lot like Vamp. Well, more like a descendant of Vamp."

"But you can go out in the sun." My mind raced, whirling through the possibilities I wished I'd had when I'd been in the city.

"I can." Walsh took my hand, leading me over to sit on his bed. "I can eat food, too."

"Then whatever you took isn't like Vamp at all. It's a cure for everybody on the outside." My whole body went numb, like my mind racing so quickly had stolen all the blood from my limbs.

"It's not a cure. There are just different tradeoffs."

"Like what?" I looked into his eyes—his brown, almost golden, eyes. Normal eyes, not the black of the vampires I'd known.

"Pheromones mostly." He held my hand. "The drug changes the way your brain works. Draws you into a pack. And once you're there, it can be hard to think like your old self anymore. Every fiber of your being calls for you to serve your leader."

"What leader, the maker? Did a maker find a way to create minions?"

"Not the maker." Walsh studied our hands. "The alpha."

"Alpha. Like wolves?"

"Right in one." Walsh let go of my hand.

"Are you..." I leaned forward, making him look at me. "Are you telling me you're a wolf?"

A line formed between Walsh's eyebrows. "People call us were-wolves, but I don't grow extra hair. I can't bite somebody to infect them."

"And the full moon?"

"Makes it harder to manage." He hunched forward, resting his elbows on his knees. "It's not that bad here, away from the pack. Honestly, most of it's better when I'm on my own. But I'm here on the alpha's orders. He gave me a mission, and I have to see it through. The chemicals in my brain won't allow me to fail him."

I dug my fingers into my hair, pulling at the roots. "This is exactly the sort of thing I should be nowhere near."

"I know. But I didn't choose to sneak in through the digital gap made for you and Mari. And I had to go after Strand tonight. He was my step one. I've spent more than a month trying to meet him. It had to be done."

"Was he really that bad?"

"He was worse than you can imagine. Thousands upon thousands of people are dead because of that man. I don't enjoy killing, Lanni. But that man had to go."

"Okay." I lifted Walsh's chin, tipping his face toward me.

He had a look in his eyes, like he really was worried I'd think he was evil for killing a kep.

"Strand had to go. I'll stay in line with the story. But whatever else you have to do, you leave me out of it. I have to keep Mari safe. I'm only here to protect her, and I can't let anyone or anything put her in danger."

"I know." Walsh touched my cheek. "I promise you, I'll keep Mari safe. You have my word."

I leaned into his hand. The horrible heat had faded from his skin, but it still had an unnatural warmth, like the sun was kissing my face.

"You should go." Walsh pulled his hand away from me and stood. "Rumors about us dating and whispers about us spending too much time alone in my room are two different beasts."

"Right." I looked to my shirt on the floor.

"I'll clean it. You aren't poison proof."

"No, I'm not." I headed for the door.

The kitchen knife sat on the counter. The blade had been tinged red with his blood.

"At the depot." I picked up the knife. "You had a cut on your head. I put styptic powder on it to stop the bleeding. Why didn't you heal then?"

"I used an anti-coagulant. Basically anti-styptic power. It hurts like hell to rub on, but it'll keep me from healing."

"But when we got here, the doctors examined all of us. Didn't they notice?"

"I can pass for a normal human as long as no one looks too closely at my blood. I had to remake my injuries every time the doctors looked away. It sucks, but I know how to make it look like I'm healing at an average speed."

"Your alpha sent you prepared." I set the knife back down.

"There's a lot riding on my success."

"Then good luck. Just keep it away from Mari and me."

I didn't say anything else before I walked out of his room. I was too scared that if I stayed, I'd never want to leave.

I made my shoulders relax before walking down the hall.

Someone was fighting against the Incorporation. Someone with enough power to do things like create werewolves.

But had the werewolves only been made to stand against the domes, or had it just been another way to survive and Walsh's pack had taken up the fight against the Incorporation? How many people were fighting beside him? How much planning had it taken to get him inside the domes? What would happen if the Arc Domes' doctors ever decided they needed to look at Walsh's blood?

The questions wouldn't stop as I crossed the bridges in the Marsh Dome and made my way back down into the concrete corridor.

How long had he been a werewolf? What was his pack's goal? How much of the glass would be left standing if Walsh succeeded?

I stopped in the staircase leading to Bloom Dome, trying to shove my thoughts into an order that would keep Mari from noticing my panic.

The Incorporation was evil. They treated everyone on the outside like disposable scum who were only born so they could die in service to the domes. I didn't know if the world would be a better place without the Incorporation in it, but I knew all too well the pain the Incorporation caused.

The kep needed to be stopped.

But if someone destroyed the Incorporation, what would happen to Mari and me?

A surge of guilt rolled through my stomach. Thousands, maybe hundreds of thousands of people suffered every day at the hands of the Incorporation. That was more important than my life could ever be.

But Mari? I'd do anything to protect her.

But if that meant helping the kep...

"Stop, Lanni. Just stop," I whispered as I climbed the rest of the stairs. "Just keep your head down and stay the hell out of it."

CHAPTER SIXTEEN

It took an hour for me to convince Miranda I hadn't been traumatized by watching Strand die and she could leave Mari and me alone.

I made sure Mari had eaten and done her schoolwork before climbing into the shower. I tried not to think about the obscene luxury as I stood in the hot water, scrubbing my whole body three times just to make sure no hint of Walsh's poison lingered on my skin.

Even when I was done washing, I couldn't convince myself to leave the safety of the shower.

Hidden somewhere warm and quiet and alone. No bodies on the ground. No secrets I didn't fully understand.

I pressed my forehead to the cool tile wall.

Images of Strand on the ground, shaking as he choked on nothing, clawed into my mind. Pain pressed on the front of my chest. My shoulders shook as I breathed in the steam.

"He was a demon. He wasn't a real person. He was only a monster. Murderers don't deserve pity."

By the time I got out of the shower, Mari had already curled up in bed and fallen asleep. I felt horrible and selfish for not making sure I tucked her in. And worse for not being able to clear my mind enough to do my schoolwork.

I curled up, sitting at the head of my bed, just staring into the darkness.

You'll be okay, Jaime's voice whispered in my mind. *You've survived so much. You'll get through this, too.*

Tears burned in my eyes. I needed Jaime. Not just as a voice in my head. I needed him with me, to hold me, to help me figure out which way was up and what I should do.

I needed to tell him that werewolves existed. I needed to spend hours talking through the whole mess with him. And once we'd figured it out, I needed to curl up in his arms and sleep, knowing I was protected, because Jaime and I always took care of each other.

I gripped the covers beneath me, trying to convince my tears to stay silent, but the pain in my chest just kept getting worse.

I crept over to Mari's bed, making sure she really was asleep, then headed out into the hall.

The corridor lights had been turned to their dim evening setting. Not that it really mattered. There wasn't anyone else around.

I paused outside Harper's door, testing myself, making sure I was broken enough to need her, and strong enough to lie, before knocking.

It only took a moment for Harper to open the door. She leaned against the wall, studying my face for a long moment.

"That bad?" she whispered.

"I watched Strand die."

"Shit." Harper opened her door all the way, letting me into her room.

The space was almost identical to the room I shared with Mari, but Harper only had one bed, and she wasn't as careful about making sure nothing was out of place.

Her dinner dishes still waited in the sink, her dirty clothes hadn't made it into her designated laundry bag, and her bed hadn't been made.

Neither of us spoke until Harper had closed the door behind me.

"Sit," Harper said. "You look like you're about to pass out."

"It's been a really shitty day." I took one of the two chairs at Harper's table.

"I heard Strand had died. I didn't know you'd been there." She pulled two glasses out of her cabinet.

"Yeah, he was tonight's assignment for *chat with an elder* time."

"How did it happen?" She set the glasses on the table before going to dig in her closet.

"He was talking about how wonderful he was and all the ways he'd helped the Incorporation. Then he stopped talking, fell, twitched, and died."

"Shit." Harper came back with a jug like the ones we'd used to collect our water rations in the city. "Was it just you?"

"Walsh was there, too."

Harper set the jug down and pursed her lips. "Would have been better if you were in a crowd, but at least there was someone else who can back you up."

"Back me up?"

"Yep." Harper opened the jug. A sharp, sweet scent filled the air. "Or haven't you heard? Someone bombed the medical corridor."

"You know I've heard."

"But now the rumors have gone from whispers behind closed doors to brazen talk in the halls." Harper poured the cloudy golden liquid into each of our cups. "There's a traitor in the Arc Domes. Someone is working against the Incorporation."

I gripped my cup, concentrating on the feel of the glass in my hand rather than the hundred different ways I should be panicking.

"To shit days." Harper raised her cup to me.

I took a sip. I recognized the sting of the liquor in the back of my throat.

Jaime and I had tried gin someone had traded him in the market. We'd laughed at how awful it had tasted.

I took another sip, not caring that the flavor was a horrific blend of sweet and sour.

"So, what's the Incorporation going to do?" I asked once I was sure I wasn't going to cough.

"Investigate." Harper shrugged. "I don't know what they're looking into, that's way above my position, but they're already digging around. And an original team member dropping dead… that'll only make things worse."

"They think he was killed?"

"No idea. But I'm sure someone will be paranoid enough to start asking questions. And we don't want anyone looking at you."

I took too big a sip and coughed as the liquor burned my throat.

"You don't like my home-made wine?" Harper laughed.

"Is that what this is supposed to be?"

"Don't knock it." Harper poured herself a second glass. "It took me forever to figure out how to brew something this good. The Incorporation doesn't exactly endorse alcohol consumption, let alone home brewing."

"It's great. I'm just not used to it."

"It's not great. But it tastes a lot better than having feelings." Harper clinked her glass against mine.

We sat in silence for a long moment, Harper staring into her glass, me battling with myself over whether or not I should tell her about Walsh.

Alec and Harper had gotten Mari and me into the Arc Domes. Harper was the closest thing to a real friend I had inside the glass. If I told her about Walsh, she couldn't turn him in, not without risking Mari and me. Better to tell her about Walsh than Walsh about Harper.

Better not to tell anyone anything.

I coughed as I took another sip.

"You don't have to finish it," Harper said.

"I don't want to be rude."

"Leaving more for me isn't rude. I think I'm going to experiment with different fruits for the next batch. Might as well, right?"

"Sure." I didn't argue as Harper reached across the table and took my glass. "Are you okay?"

"Me?" Harper raised an eyebrow. "I actually made it to the Arc Domes. I'm driving the safest route the apocalypse has to offer. I live in a place with a fucking manmade beach. What more could I ask for?"

"Lots of things." I took Harper's hand. "Not to have someone planting bombs inside the domes would be a great start."

Harper dragged her free hand over her head, ruffling her short, red hair. "I just keeping feeling like the bottom's going to fall out and everything's going to go to hell."

"Why?"

"I'm finally on my own. I'm out of the Plains Domes. It's just...people like me don't get to be happy. Something's going to screw it up."

I stood and cut around to Harper's side of the table. I wrapped my arms around her, holding her close to my side like I would have done with Mari. Like Jaime would have done for me.

"The world is a dark and shitty place. And, yeah, we're living trapped in glass with people who like to build bombs. But if you're happy, even for a second, you're winning." I squeezed her tighter. "And if things start to go wrong, you're not going to be on your own. You saved Mari and me. I have your back, Harper."

"I should have known Amery's kids would be good people. Even if they didn't know him." Harper gave me a quick hug around the middle before grabbing the jug to refill both glasses.

I pretended not to notice her brushing her tears away.

"You really like Amery that much?" I didn't fight as Harper pressed a glass into my hand. I took a drink, almost grateful for the fire that burned away the knot in my throat.

"Yeah." Harper pulled my chair closer to me with her foot. "He helped me get here."

"Was that the deal you made, for helping Mar and me?"

"Yeah. I'd been eyeing a transfer since I was in school, but the Plains Domes Council wasn't going to approve it."

"Why?" I sat back in my chair, studying Harper's face as she stared into her glass.

"Gender balance. They were happy to send Alec and some of the other male guards over, but they didn't want to let any of the females go. Women are considered too valuable an asset to even consider trading us away." Harper ran her finger along the rim of her cup. "I thought I was never going to be able to get out. I even considered stealing a van and just driving as far as the gas would take me. Seeing how long I could survive on my own."

"It was that bad?" I took another drink, moving slowly so I wouldn't jar Harper out of whatever memory kept her gaze fixed on her glass.

"Yeah. It really was. Amery lived in the same housing dome as me. He'd known me since I was little. And I drove for the guards, so he'd see me at work. He was the only one to notice how bad it had gotten and how much I really needed to get out. He called in so many favors, even went in front of the Council to petition for my transfer. When they approved it, I asked if I could do anything for him. He told me about you and Mari and asked me to help. I told him we had a deal."

"He helped you first, before you promised him anything?"

"That's Amery." Harper's hand shook as she took another drink.

"Why do so many people owe him favors?"

"Because he's a good guy who's been bending the rules to help people for a long time. Someone like Amery saves you, you'd kill for him. No questions asked." Harper downed the rest of her glass.

I swallowed what was left in mine, letting the wine burn all the way down to my stomach, singeing away the ache growing in my gut because I'd never met the man who'd helped so many people.

"Is it really that different here?" I asked. "You're still living inside glass, and the Incorporation's still in charge."

"Yeah. It's different."

She didn't say anything else as she poured us another round. We just settled into the silence. Both of us drinking, both of us staring into our glasses.

I wished I could tell Harper about Walsh.

I just couldn't shake the feeling that whatever she wasn't telling me might be even bigger.

CHAPTER SEVENTEEN

My head pounded like my blood wanted to shatter my skull, and my throat was dry enough to make swallowing painful when I woke up early the next morning. I ignored the dehydration as I got out of bed to check the computer screen set into the wall.

PAM didn't have any notices for me. I pressed my forehead against the wall, grateful that, at the very least, I wouldn't have to start my first day of the training program with a hangover.

I poured myself a glass of water and sat on my bed, watching Mari sleep. She was so sweet, so innocent. Just a little girl who deserved a chance to live a safe and happy life.

I had to protect her.

Harper would help me. Alec would help me. Even Walsh would help me.

I am lucky.

I woke Mari up, and she chatted as we got ready for school. She made a fuss about eating her breakfast, only taking a bite for each bite I ate. I loved her for it. For forcing me to eat.

Walking through the tunnels was easier with Mari. I could keep my attention fixed on her and ignore the people around us.

I gave her a hug and a kiss on the head outside her classroom, and then I was alone in a sea of kep. Surrounded by people experience had taught me to hate.

I am lucky. I am lucky.

I tried to concentrate on the joy of having a full stomach as I walked by the Haven Dome. I passed a pack of guards in the hall and tried to remember they weren't my enemy. It was their job to keep Mari safe.

My boots kept my feet safe. The humming air filtration system kept my lungs safe.

I gripped my tablet.

"Lanni." Gideon pushed away from the wall where he'd been leaning, walking in the opposite direction of our classroom to get to me. "How are you?"

"Fine." I loosened my grip on my tablet and made my shoulders relax.

"My dad mentioned you were with Strand last night," Gideon said. "I'm sorry. That can't have been an easy thing."

"I'm a little shaken up, but I'll survive."

Gideon glanced over his shoulder, toward our classroom.

I wondered if I'd said the wrong thing. Would a kep girl have wept because they'd watched a stranger die? I'd seen too many kep-made corpses in my life to know what parts of death should be frightening.

"I know this is terrible timing after what you went through last night." Gideon tucked his hands into his pockets. "And *no* is a fine answer. But I was thinking about what Mr. Lewis said about how they used to dance up in the atrium, and I had my dad bring it to the Council. They didn't approve anything huge, but they have agreed to a few hours of music."

"That's great."

"I think it could be a really fun night." Gideon stopped talking as Walsh walked by.

Walsh lingered near the classroom door. A regular human

would have been too far away to hear, but from the way he stood, it looked like Walsh was listening to every word.

"So"—Gideon bounced on his toes—"since we both heard about it together, I was wondering if you'd want to go with me. I mean, I don't know anything about dancing, but I thought we could have fun."

"Oh."

Walsh nodded like he was agreeing with something he was reading on his tablet.

"Sure." I pressed my face into a smile. "Do you know when it's going to be? I'm supposed to have more things assigned to my schedule. I'm getting put into the guard training program."

"Yeah." Gideon's whole body seemed to bounce as he nodded again. "Those sessions are mostly in the morning. And they won't conflict, I asked my dad."

"How does he know?" I headed toward the classroom, waving for Gideon to come with me.

"Right, sorry. I'm not used to people not knowing who he is." Pink tinged Gideon's cheeks. "My dad's Captain Pace. He's the head of the Outer Guard. You met him in your Council meeting. He's the one who added you to the program."

"He seemed nice." I didn't let myself look at Walsh as I passed by him to go up the stairs. "Honestly, I thought I would get a lot worse for punching a guard."

Gideon laughed. "You might have, but I don't know many people who haven't wanted to punch Guard Kealy. You just got to live out the rest of our dreams."

"How lucky am I?" I spoke a little louder as we passed Mrs. Hale. "You'll let me know when the dance is, right? I don't want to miss it."

"Sure," Gideon said. "PAM's going to make an announcement, but I thought maybe we could meet up before the music starts. Take a walk or something."

"Sounds great." I slipped into my seat. "I've learned where all the domes are, but I bet there are a bunch of beautiful things I haven't found yet."

"Right. I'll think of something good." Gideon beamed and bounced his way to his desk.

Mrs. Hale looked like she might burst with joy as she called our class to order.

We were fifteen minutes into the lesson when I caught Walsh glancing my way. He gave me another tiny nod, like we were part of the same team trying to work on the same plan.

Something about it eased the pounding in my head and made walking to the Tropics Dome less daunting, and standing in the humid air, staring at the plants that should never have grown in the mountains, while listening to the calls of the monkeys that hid just out of sight, didn't fill me with horrible, disgusting self-loathing.

I knew I was lying to myself. I wasn't working against the Incorporation. I had accepted their protection. My complacency made me guilty, a collaborator with the enemy that had made my life hell. But even if I wasn't a part of Walsh's secret plans, I'd helped. By screaming when he told me to and keeping my mouth shut, I'd helped a werewolf kill a monster.

That had to count for something. In the grand balance of my life, Strand's death had to cancel out some of the guilt I bore for living inside the glass.

It was nowhere near absolution, but that thought was enough to actually make me hungry for dinner. And I didn't have to force myself to laugh while Mari told me about her day.

PAM dinged with a message telling me to report to a far corner of the domes in the morning for training, and I didn't panic.

It was stupid and naïve, but a little voice in the back of my head was eager to learn to fight. Just in case.

In case Walsh needed me again.

CHAPTER EIGHTEEN

The early morning glow sparkled on the glass in a way I'd never seen at night, bathing Bloom Dome in a warm golden gleam that made it look more like a fairytale forest than ever. I cut away from the path to the stairs, stepping over flowerbeds and weaving between trees to reach the glass.

Far below the domes, mist covered the forest and crept up the mountainsides. The sun had risen over the peaks to the east, but the angle of the light left shadows on the faraway slopes that made them look sharp and daring, like they were sentinels guarding the Arcadia Domes instead of massive mounds of rock locking me away from the world.

There was no hint that anyone outside the glass existed. For a moment, I didn't mind the isolation.

The early morning offered peace and solitude.

No wonder Strand loved it.

I searched myself for some regret that he'd died. That I'd been a part of his murder, even if my role hadn't begun until after the fact.

I couldn't find any sorrow, shock, or shame. Just a bit of pride I wasn't sure a sane person should feel.

Cold trickled into my gut.

"He was a monster." I pressed my palms to the glass, trying not to slip into self-loathing for still having a tiny hint of doubt I couldn't get to go away. "He was a murderer. He helped the kep slaughter innocent people. Anyone with a conscience would be glad he's gone. You're not broken."

I crept back to the path and headed down the stairs. The corridors were almost empty as I made my way through the tunnels toward the guards' barracks.

I passed a few workers from the cleaning crews and could hear soft chatter from people walking just far enough ahead of me I couldn't see them in the curved tunnels.

Without the normal bustle of kep, it was almost possible to forget I lived surrounded by demons. Not for long, just a second. Just long enough for me to take a full breath without guilt pressing against my lungs.

For that one second, the walls of the corridor were clean and perfect, a promise for a bright and plentiful future. Then reality came crashing back down, and horror dripped from the lights and slicked the floors.

Calm down, Lanni.

The chatter ahead of me got louder as I neared the barracks, and by the time I could finally see the people who were talking, fifteen students had gathered at the meeting point.

I recognized a few of them from class. Gideon, Walsh, Elliot, and a girl I was pretty sure was named Tricia. There were a few other faces I recognized from around the domes, too. Kids from other classes who I'd only ever passed in the halls.

Only one person wore a black guard's uniform, and it wasn't Captain Pace. This guard was younger, probably only in his twenties, but he stared at the teens in front of him like he was the king of the kep and we were all lowly factory filth.

I tucked my hands into my pockets to keep from curling them into fists. Punching one guard in the face had gotten me into the training program. I couldn't imagine I'd get off as easily if I punched a second guard.

Walsh gave me a nod as I joined the group. I'd been aiming to stand near him, but he glanced toward Gideon, so I weaved farther into the pack to stand there instead.

"Lanni." Gideon gave me a sleepy smile. "Are you ready for this?"

"I have no idea." I shrugged. "But I have to be here, so yeah, I'll be fine."

Elliot looked back toward me. "You didn't apply for the program?"

"Her acceptance came straight from my dad," Gideon said. "She's going to be great."

Elliot looked forward again.

"Thanks." I mouthed to Gideon.

"Eyes front," the guard said.

The group went silent as we all faced him.

"We're taking the long route to the vehicle bay. Keep up." The guard turned and started running up the corridor the way I'd come.

"Fun," I whispered to myself before joining the pack chasing the guard.

It wasn't a sprint, by any means. It was the sort of steady pace I'd kept to when I'd needed to run from the trade hall all the way to our apartment—fast enough to get where I was going without trouble catching up, slow enough to be able to make it the whole way.

When the kep stormed the hall to crack down on water trades or whatever other thing they'd decided we weren't allowed to do, I'd sprint away, tearing through the night and not stopping until I was so out of breath I couldn't move anymore. Then I'd hide in the shadows and catch my breath so I could sprint another stretch. Hiding and bolting, hiding and bolting, until I could make it all the way home.

I'd been so caught up in thinking about home, I hadn't noticed I was right on the guard's heels.

Too fast, Lanni. Be good enough to stay, not good enough to be recruited as a guard, a voice that sounded like Alec's spoke in my head.

I didn't like it. I didn't want his voice in my thoughts. Alec didn't belong there.

It didn't make his advice any less reasonable.

I took a few gasping breaths and dropped farther back in the pack, like I hadn't known how to pace myself and had pushed too hard.

Walsh ran just ahead of the middle of the group. I wanted to know how fast a werewolf could run with no one holding him back. But if he could pretend to be near the middle, I could fake being at the end.

I fell farther back, running at the end of the cluster of people but ahead of the two boys that had fallen behind and puffed along in our wake.

We did a full round of the lower corridors, cutting through maintenance halls to complete the circle, before going to the stairs. The guard ran us up and down the steps twice before continuing into the corridors on the next level. We didn't do a full round on that level. The guard cut a strange path, keeping us away from the damaged medical corridor.

I stared at the back of the guard's head, wishing I could reach in and pluck out whatever information he knew about the investigation into the bomber.

I'd seen kep tear city scum's homes apart, searching for whatever stupid thing they'd decided outsiders shouldn't have. I couldn't picture the guards being so forgiving about losing supplies, not even if the damage had been done by one of their own.

But, as far as I could see, the guards were content to let their investigation creep quietly along. Someone had planted a bomb, and the Incorporation cared more about maintaining the placid perfection of the domes than finding the damn traitor.

Harper had said they were searching for the bomber. I didn't have enough faith in the guards or the Incorporation to let the vague concept of their investigation comfort me when the person responsible was still wandering around the Arc Domes. I'd have happily torn through kep homes looking for evidence if it wouldn't have gotten me tossed out of the domes. How were the Dome Guard not breaking down doors to find the bomber who'd endangered us all?

I'd finally started to get truly out of breath when the guard ran us through the thick metal doors that led into the bay. I'd never been allowed in there before, and even though I'd known it was where they stored all of the Arc Domes' land vehicles, I hadn't expected the space to be so massive.

The ceiling was thirty feet high. The concrete room was long enough to fit the twenty-five trucks parked along either side and the vans and construction equipment farther back. I couldn't see any hint of the Arc Domes' helicopters.

The center of the room had been left as an open space, though it seemed strange for any place inside the glass to have extra room that hadn't been taken over by plants. The sound of our panting as we all tried to catch our breath seemed unwelcome, like the concrete didn't want any living things around.

"You okay?" Walsh whispered to me.

"Who doesn't love running through halls?" I said.

"I meant in here." Walsh glanced toward the trucks. "It's a lot like the depot."

I hadn't realized it until he said it. Or maybe some part of me had started to feel the combination of fear and dread, and I just had too many chemicals from the run pumping through my brain to notice.

My pulse started racing in a different way. My hands shook as I pushed back the stray hairs that had fallen loose around my face.

"I'm fine." I fought the urge to run home and make sure Mari was still safely in bed. "Ceiling is solid here, so you don't even have to worry about it shattering and slicing me. I'd hate to have to ask you to dig glass out of my arm again."

Walsh squeezed my hand. "You ever get sliced up, you come straight to me. I'll patch you up anytime."

All I could do was nod. If I tried to say how much it helped to have someone who had my back that understood the world I'd come from, I'd start crying in the middle of the bay.

"We're going to do a full circuit of physical training before moving on to hand-to-hand combat," the guard said. "And if you think today is hard, you're going to break when Captain Pace takes over your training next month. This is kid stuff. Basics. My job is to get you ready for Pace. He'll be the one to turn you into Outer Guard material, am I understood?"

"Yes, sir," some of the group shouted.

"I said, am I understood?"

"Yes, sir." I joined in with the rest.

"Then form a line."

By the time we'd finished with the physical training, my muscles had started to shake. Before we'd gotten through the basic fighting stances and worked on the proper technique for punching the air, I knew I'd be limping on the way home.

One of the boys from the back of the running pack started crying when the guard finally told us to go home and shower. One of the others had gone so pale, I didn't think he'd be able to walk home on his own.

I rested my hands on top of my head, trying to get the blood to drain back out of my throbbing fingers, and headed for the bay doors that led back into the corridors of the domes.

"So, what did you think?" Gideon still had a bounce in his step even though he was covered in sweat.

"That getting put on a maintenance detail as guard-punching punishment would have been easier," I said. "And honestly, why does your dad want to teach me to punch with greater accuracy and force? Doesn't that seem like an awful idea?"

Gideon laughed, like he genuinely thought I was being funny. "Dad likes meaningful consequences. He comes up with the weirdest stuff. Made me go without socks for a week once because I'd left a pair on the floor of my room."

"How'd that work out?"

"I gained a greater appreciation for socks and never left any of my clothes out again." Gideon bowed me through the bay doors.

"Don't want to risk having to walk around the domes pantsless?"

"I don't know if Dad would go quite that far." Red crept up Gideon's cheeks.

"I suppose pantsless would be disruptive to the order of the domes." I sighed as we reached the bottom of the stairs I had to climb to get home. Gritting my teeth against the ache in my legs, I started up the steps.

"So, the announcement is going to go out later." Gideon matched my slow pace as some of the others cut around us. "The dance is going to be tomorrow night."

"Dancing." I winced as my legs screamed at me. "If I'm not so sore I can't walk, that could be fun."

"I was thinking I could maybe come by an hour early," Gideon said. "I could show you some of the Arc Domes' hidden gems."

Keep them happy. Be a normal girl.

"Let me make sure Mari can go to our guardian's," I said. "I don't like leaving her alone."

"How old is she?" Gideon asked.

"Seven." We reached the top of the stairs, but he kept walking with me. I didn't know if he lived in the same direction or was just walking me home. "She wouldn't mind being on her own. She's old for her age."

"I guess she's had to be." Gideon furrowed his brow. "You both have."

"Yeah. We have." It came out harsher than I'd meant it to.

Gideon winced. "I'm sorry. I shouldn't have said that."

"It's fine." I gave him the best smile I could manage. "We just try not to talk about before. Our life started when we got on the caravan to come here. Everything before that doesn't matter anymore."

We walked in silence for a minute.

"For whatever it's worth," Gideon said as we reached the stairs to Bloom Dome, "I'm glad you're here."

"Thanks. I'm glad you were waiting for me." I gave Gideon a nod before limping up the steps.

He had a look on his face like I'd just handed him the most precious gift he'd ever been offered.

Too far. Too far.

The guilt in my stomach was swallowed by something darker.

He'll never be Jaime.

CHAPTER NINETEEN

"It's the prettiest color." Mari held up my blue shirt.

"But this one shows off her"—Harper looked to me, my charcoal gray shirt in hand—"features better."

"Do I really need to worry about showing off my *features*?" I dragged a brush through my hair.

"The human race managed to destroy the environment but not the patriarchy." Harper threw the charcoal shirt at me. "Your teacher was desperate enough to set you up on blind dates. Make yourself pretty for the boys and get Mrs. *I like to be grossly inappropriate while interfering in my students' lives* Hale off your back."

"Fair point." I pulled on the charcoal shirt and looked at myself in the mirror.

If I'd been going out back home in the city, heading to the Misery Drain, actually wanting to dance, I'd have found what passed for makeup in the non-essential stores to darken my eyes and lips and chosen a shirt that cut a good two inches lower in the front.

But makeup didn't exist in the domes, and the clothes I had were what Miranda had gathered from the warehouse below the domes. So brushed hair and a shirt that hugged my chest were the extent of what was expected.

"You look beautiful." Mari flopped down onto the bed beside me. "I wish I could go."

"Me too, Mar." I bent down and kissed the top of her head.

"Do you think they'll play music when kids can go?" Mari asked.

"Don't count on it," Harper said. "Only the young and unmarried are invited to this party, because that's not obvious at all."

"What do you mean?" I froze, half-bent over to get my boots.

"It's not just Mrs. Hale freaking out about you finding a boyfriend." Harper hopped up to sit on our kitchen counter. "The Arc Domes lost a lot of guards when the River Domes fell. They should have gotten more in the citizen swap, but our caravan was slaughtered at the depot."

"That's why they started the guard training program." I sat and yanked on my boots.

"Just a temporary stopgap," Harper said. "The Incorporation always plays the long game. What they need is more citizens. That means breeding. If the overseers living at the top of our mountain are crossing their fingers and hoping our age group will cheerfully breed sooner, they have to pair us off younger."

An odd, crawling chill wormed its way up my arms. "Then I hope some people fall in love and sneak into the shadows without protection tonight."

"Yep, you do," Harper said. "Other people's mistakes will keep you and me safe."

"Safe from what?" A crease pinched between Mari's eyebrows.

"Having to go to even more stupid dances." I tied my boots, keeping my gaze fixed on my laces rather than risk Mari reading the fear in my eyes. "Are you coming tonight, Harper?"

"I have neither enough wine nor the will to survive the necessary hangover," Harper said. "I'll walk Mari to Miranda's and hide in my room with the lights off until it's over."

"You're lucky you don't have a Mrs. Hale chasing you down." I stood up and checked my hair in the mirror one more time.

"Real lucky," Harper said. "Come on, Mari. Let's get out of here before Gideon shows up."

"But I want to meet him," Mari said.

"You can meet him some other time," Harper said. "It's better if we're not here. Trust me. You're lucky if you can dodge some kinds of grownup stuff."

"Fine." Mari gave me a tight hug. "But I get to meet him soon."

"Okay." I gave Mari a squeeze. "I'll make sure you do."

Harper chivvied Mari out of our room, and I just stood still, like I was stuck in a moment in time that I should have been smart enough to use to run away.

"He's not a vampire, he's a seventeen-year-old boy. Stop freaking out."

I paced the center of our room, trying to get my legs to stop aching with each step. The second day of the guard training program hadn't been any easier than the first.

We'd run, done strength training, worked on basic self-defense. I'd been sore enough that faking being a slow runner had been a relief.

I froze at a timid knock on our door.

"Lanni," Gideon called softly.

"Coming." I shimmied down the neckline of my shirt and opened the door.

Gideon had tamed his hair and put on a crisp blue shirt. Pink crept up his cheeks as he gave me a nod that bordered on a bow. "Are you ready?"

"Sure." I closed the door behind me. A weird jolt of fear shot through my lungs like I'd just locked myself out of safety.

"So, I figured out where I want to take you," Gideon said. "It's a little walking tour of sorts."

"Sounds great." I headed toward the front door of my building.

"Please don't get too excited. Honestly, I spent, like, two hours trying to think through what the best things to show you might be. Some of the most unique things about the Arc Domes are pretty obvious."

"You mean the fact that there's a beach?"

"Yeah." Gideon darted in front of me to open the door.

"Thanks." I tipped my head, letting my hair hide my face from him.

I wasn't sure if I was supposed to take his hand, or blush, or…I didn't even know what all the *ors* should be. Leisurely evening dates had never been a thing in my world. I'd only ever flirted if I needed something or was trying to protect myself.

"I decided to skip over the really obvious choices." Gideon turned away from the path that led out of Bloom Dome, heading instead toward the fountain at the dead center of the space. "I've spent enough time hiding around here to know some really beautiful places people aren't likely to find."

"Why were you hiding?"

He didn't answer right away. The sound of our footsteps joined the soft chirps of the birds settling into their nests for the night and the gentle rustling of the water in the fountain.

"Captain Pace is my dad," Gideon said.

"I know."

"Did you notice how big he is? The man is a mountain."

"I mean, he was sitting, but he did look like he belonged in the guards."

Gideon cut right, along a path lined by trees with white blooms.

"I have three older brothers the same size as my dad." Gideon raised his hand like he was going to run his fingers through his hair before catching himself and tucking his hands into his pockets. "I'm the runt."

"The runt? Like an animal?" I couldn't keep the laughter from my voice.

"Basically." Gideon gave a rueful chuckle. "I didn't even get this tall until last year. And before I finally managed to put on some muscle six months ago, my brothers could pick me up and toss me around whenever they got bored. Mom's in medical. Dad's a guard. They never had time to make sure my brothers didn't do too much damage, so I got really good at hiding. Saved me a lot of bruises."

"I'm sorry. Your brothers shouldn't have done that to you."

"Siblings. It is what it is."

I touched his arm to stop his stride. "If anyone tried to hurt my sister, I'd kill them. Being related is not an excuse for being an asshole. Life can be shitty sometimes, but hurting someone just for fun, it's never okay."

"Thanks." He laid his hand on top of mine.

The warmth of his touch didn't make me want to scream.

"Show me this hiding place." I let his fingers linger on mine for a moment as I lifted my hand away.

"Careful not to step on the flowers." Gideon led me down a side path, over a bed of white blooms, and into the mulch beyond.

I followed him, holding a hand above my head to protect my hair as we ducked below tree branches.

"Lanni, I didn't tell you that so you'd feel sorry for me."

"I believe you."

"Good."

We weaved between trees, cutting away from the houses hidden behind their leaves.

He stopped beside a willow tree, lifting the branches aside like he was pulling back a curtain. "Welcome to the Woodland Palace. Also known as stop one on the *my brothers are assholes* tour."

I laughed, a very small but real laugh, as I ducked under the drooping branches.

The layers of leaves circled around us, leaving a hollow where

Gideon and I stood. The glow of the dome barely penetrated our safety, giving enough light to see by, but still letting me pretend the rest of the world had somehow disappeared.

"Wow."

"You're not disappointed?" Gideon sat on a thick, curving branch that grew off the side of the tree.

"No. This is beautiful." I ran my fingers along the tree's bark. The wood was firm. It felt healthy, almost like it wanted to prove it was alive.

The trees in the city hadn't been like that. They'd always looked closer to rotting than thriving.

"It's hard to find a place in the domes where you can really feel alone," Gideon said.

"Have you..." I sat beside Gideon, leaving a few inches of space between us. "Have you ever thought about what it would be like, if you weren't trapped in the domes?"

"Sure. I think everyone's wished they were born a few hundred years in the future. To be a part of the generation that will get to step out into a healthy world and rebuild life as it should be. If I could trade places and be one of them, that would be the dream."

"I don't mean the out there that will be. I mean living out in the world now." I tipped my head to look at him.

He watched my hair fall over my shoulder, a cascade of black even kep envied.

"There is nothing out there." Gideon planted his hands on his knees. "All that exists outside the glass is death."

"There are people that live out there now. Working in factories, trying to survive. Parents and brothers and kids. Have you ever thought about what it would be like, to be out there with them?"

"I can't. They're them. We're us. Two different things best kept apart."

"Right." I dug my nails into the tree's bark as I looked up. I couldn't even see the glass above us through the branches.

"Do you think about it? What it would be like to live out there?"

"Always. I can't stop thinking about it. The ones who are hungry, and sick, and scared. I feel so trapped in here, but we're the lucky ones."

Gideon took my hand. "We are the lucky ones. That doesn't mean you can't feel trapped, and it doesn't mean you're not allowed to feel compassion."

"But you said—"

"I'm going to be an Outer Guard, Lanni. It was decided as soon as I was born. Feeling sorry for outsiders and wondering what their lives are like could get me and my fellow guards killed. But just because I can't think about outsiders that way doesn't mean it's wrong. Though, it may mean being an Outer Guard isn't for you."

"I think you're right." I laced my fingers through his. "Just don't tell anyone. Definitely don't tell your dad until after he's forgiven me for the whole punching thing."

"It'll be our secret." Gideon looked down at our hands. "Want to visit the next stop on this tour?"

"I like it here. Let's just sit for a while."

I looked back up at the tree, trying to enjoy the way the branches drooped around us instead of wondering where I would be in that moment if I hadn't been torn away from my life outside the glass.

CHAPTER TWENTY

The music from the atrium trickled into the stairwell. It sounded like old music, from long before the world crumbled, with horns and a melody that seemed suited for sweeping around a ballroom. The music didn't fit with the concrete stairwell, but somehow the contrast made stepping up into the atrium feel like we'd been transported far away from the prison of the domes.

They'd dimmed the lights, leaving the trees around the edges of the glass as barely more than silhouettes. The sounds of laughter and chatting filtered over the music, most of it coming from by the pond where the children usually played.

"This is way better than I'd hoped it would be." Gideon beamed.

"It was your idea, and you didn't think it would be great?" I nudged him with my elbow.

"I didn't think it would be great *because* it was my idea. Come on."

He took my hand, lacing his fingers firmly through mine before heading toward the pond. Like he wanted to make sure everyone who saw us would know we'd arrived together. That I had been claimed as his date for the night.

It was better that way. Pretending to be someone else was hard enough to do with one person. Trying to keep the act going as I switched from partner to partner...that would be too exhausting to bear.

The pack of kep beside the pond had split into groups.

A cluster of them were actually dancing to the music, and around the edges, little bunches of people had formed. They talked, laughed, took advantage of the refreshments someone had laid out on a nearby table.

The Incorporation really is desperate.

"I'm sorry if I'm horrible at this." Gideon led me into the group of dancers. "PAM helped me find some old instructional videos, but I don't know if that helped or made me worse." He placed one hand on my hip while keeping the other in his grasp.

"I don't actually know how to dance like this, either."

Gideon started swaying to the music. "Basically, you follow my lead and we try not to step on each other."

"Now I can see why Mr. Lewis misses dancing so much."

We started off slow, just swaying side-to-side, not always keeping time with the music. After the first song, Gideon got more comfortable, and we started traveling a little. By the third song, he'd grown daring enough to twirl me under his arm.

We got tangled as he tried to spin me back in, and when I ended up back in his arms, he held me closer, leaving barely any space between us.

Little wrinkles formed in the corners of his eyes as we reverted to simple swaying.

I met his gaze, staring into his eyes, trying to be the girl who'd be thinking about his lips being just inches from hers. Sweet and naïve as she wondered if he was going to lean down and kiss her or if she should be brazen enough to kiss him. An innocent girl who'd blush if someone suggested going into the shadows to explore the delights that come once kissing isn't enough.

I leaned closer to him, letting my breasts press against him, shifting my hand to touch the bare skin on the back of his neck.

I kept my breathing shallow, making sure he could feel my chest move.

One kiss. One kiss in front of everyone. Then one fight where people can hear, and I'll buy myself some freedom.

I flicked my gaze to his mouth before tipping my chin up so my lips were only a whisper from his.

He tightened his hold on me for a split second before stepping away.

"We should get something to drink." He nodded toward the table. "We've been working hard in training, and we can't risk...umm..."

"Dehydration?" I offered.

"Yeah."

Even in the dim light, I could see the red creeping into his cheeks.

"Maybe we can dance again later." I took his hand, keeping close to his side as we wound our way through the dancers toward the refreshment tables.

They'd laid out cups of water with berries in them and platters of sliced fruit and baked treats.

I took the first cup I could grab, not wanting to look at the table. Seeing the ignored bounty made pretending harder.

Gideon grabbed a cup of his own and led me toward a cluster of young men. Some of them, I recognized from the guard training program. The rest looked like they'd already joined the guards. None of them were in uniform, but they had the cropped hair and squared shoulders of people who'd been told being neat would keep them alive.

Gideon planted us opposite two boys who had his hair color and Captain Pace's build.

I leaned close to whisper in his ear. "Are those your brothers?"

"Two of them," he whispered back.

"Can I punch them?"

He leaned even closer so his cheek grazed mine. "Do you mind if I put my arm around your waist for a minute? It would do a lot more damage."

I let my lips brush his cheek as I whispered, "Do it."

I looked back toward the group, trying to catch onto the thread of the conversation.

Gideon tensed as he reached behind my back to lay his hand on my hip.

"We lost an amazing military mind," one of Gideon's brothers said. "We haven't even begun to tap into the potential of the legacy Strand left for us."

"Hopefully, we'll never need to."

I looked toward the familiar voice. Alec stood at the edge of the group, his hands tucked behind his back like he was still on duty. He glanced my way, but there was no warmth or welcome in his eyes.

"Focusing on peace doesn't leave us prepared," Gideon's brother said.

"Prepared for what?" Gideon said. "An army that doesn't exist?"

Gideon's brothers both looked at him. They didn't glare. It was a different kind of loathing, like they were being forced to acknowledge something they wished didn't exist.

"How would you know what's out there?" Gideon's second brother said. "You've never left the glass."

A flare of anger sizzled in my stomach.

"They're right." I grinned at Gideon's brothers.

They smiled back like I'd just offered to go into the shadows and see how quickly we could make a new citizen for the Incorporation.

I leaned closer to Gideon, trying to hide my shudder. "I mean, you two have almost been blown up, right?"

"No." His brothers glanced between each other.

"Oh, sorry." I tipped my head, letting my hair tumble over my shoulder, displaying the side of my neck. "But you've fought without backup, right? Just you and your wits against a pack of vampires?"

"What are you talking about?" Gideon's first shit brother said.

"I'm talking about nightmare-level chaos you don't understand," I said. "So maybe don't hope for blood unless you know what the consequences look like. Guard Quinn is right. Peace is a hell of a lot better than being surrounded by corpses, so stop pounding your chests and listen to someone who's actually been there."

"Guard Quinn has seen a lot more action than—"

"I wasn't talking about him," I cut across Gideon's second shit brother. "I was talking about me. My little sister and I almost got blown up on our way here. I had to kill someone with a fucking knife to keep us alive. Violence is not fucking fun."

I didn't realize I was shaking until Gideon tightened his hold on my waist.

"Let's go." Shit brother one nodded to shit brother two.

The group stayed silent as the two of them lumbered off to nurture their scabbed manhoods.

A few others from the group left, too, letting our circle tighten until Alec stood right beside me.

"Honestly, we're lucky here," one of the others said.

"Are you okay?" Gideon whispered in my ear.

"Yeah." I nodded. "Just amazed you survived having such shit brothers."

"The hiding came in really handy." Gideon moved his arm from around my waist and took my hand.

"It's an impossible situation," the only other girl in the group said.

"Not so impossible," one of the boys said. "It's just a matter of the path of least resistance."

I tried to catch up to the conversation.

"Do you mind if I leave you for just a minute?" Gideon spoke under the rest of them. "Paul has a tendency to punch walls when he's pissed. My mom's home right now. I want to warn her."

"Good to know he's an asshole to inanimate objects, too," I said. "Go on. I'll be here."

"Thanks." He gave my hand a squeeze before hurrying away.

"Not going with him?" Alec nodded after Gideon like he thought I should follow.

"He'll be right back," I said.

"As much as I want to serve the Incorporation in a command capacity," the girl said, "I'd never want to be the one making those sorts of decisions."

"It's really a simple cost-benefit analysis," one of the boys said. "You have to think of it as an equation."

"But weighing the lives of workers versus the usefulness of the goods they produce could leave a lot of blood on your hands," the girl said.

Everything in my body tensed. I tucked my hands into my pockets to hide their shaking.

"See, the problem is you're thinking of the factory rats as living humans," another boy said. "They have no real life expectancy. You're not taking anything from them. Culling the useless population really borders on the edge of mercy."

"Walk away, Lanni."

I heard Alec's whisper, but I couldn't get my feet to move.

"Take where Alec's from," the first boy said. "They just had to purge fifty-seven percent of the population of the city serving the Plains Domes."

The trees started to sway. The music sounded hollow and tinny.

"Anyone not employed in the factories or not abiding by the

domes' orders"—the boy snapped his fingers—"gone. Why? Because they were doomed to die, and the people in the Plains Domes have to be protected at all costs. The blood of a few factory rats means nothing."

A screaming started in the very back of my mind. A high-pitched noise. I couldn't recognize who the voice belonged to.

"Breathe." Alec wrapped his arm around my waist, facing away from the group almost like he wanted to kiss me.

I tried to speak, but I couldn't push any words past the horrible pain in my throat.

"Three minutes," Alec whispered. "After all you've done to protect Mari, you can hold it together for three minutes. Right?"

I nodded.

"You must be sorry you missed that operation, Alec," the boy said. "It's not often guards get the chance to dive in and really do the work of the Incorporation."

I couldn't breathe. My lungs wouldn't inflate.

"Actually, it's pretty awful," Alec said. "If you'd ever been there, you'd know that. Let's dance, Lanni. I didn't come here for barracks talk."

He didn't loosen his hold on my waist as he led me to the dance floor.

There were people dancing and laughing, but they were all blurry. Like ghosts or demons come to haunt me.

Fifty-seven percent.

The screaming in my head got louder.

"We'll just walk through the middle." Alec's voice cut through the horrible scream. "Walk calmly to the stairs. We just have to get out of here. I believe in you, Lanni. You can make it. We just have to get out of here."

Somehow, my feet kept moving. Somehow, I managed to pull my hand from my pocket. I reached for Alec's free hand. I needed something to hold onto.

The feel of his palm pressed against mine didn't make the screaming any better.

The bright lights of the stairwell dug into my eyes. The white of them seemed absurd, like their glare was meant to burn away all the Incorporation's imperfections.

But the kep didn't think murder was wrong. The factory rats were the dirty ones.

Disposable. Useless. Unworthy of life.

A sob cracked through the pain in my throat. The sound echoed in the stairwell.

"Shh. Just keep walking. We're almost there. You can do this."

He held me so tight, he almost lifted me down the rest of the stairs.

A few people lingered in the corridor.

I looked down at Alec's hand in mine, focusing on the feel of touching a real, living human rather than let my mind create the corpses that should have filled the halls.

Thousands. Thousands and thousands of bodies. A true display of the cost of the domes.

Blood covering everything. My boots. The lights. Blood painting the walls. Dripping over everything. Filling my lungs.

My breath had started hitching in my chest, coming in unnatural gasps by the time we made it down to the level where I lived.

"Almost there. You're okay. We're almost there."

Mari.

Mari would know something was wrong. Mari could never know what the kep had done to our city. It was too much weight for me to bear. I couldn't put it on her shoulders.

Alec stopped at the steps to the Salt Dome.

"We'll be safe in here." He helped me up the stairs.

A coughing sob broke through the pain in my chest, slicing away the little bit of strength I had left.

Alec scooped me into his arms as my legs gave out. He cradled me close as I wept and the screaming in my head blocked out all sense, and reason, and anything beyond the horrible pain.

Mom. Jaime. The people I'd abandoned. Not worthy of life. Useless. Slaughtered on a whim.

CHAPTER TWENTY-ONE

I don't know how long I wept. I lost all sense of time and reason as the horrible grief and pain flooded out of me.

When the tears finally slowed, my throat was raw, my ribs hurt, and my eyes were swollen. Alec still held me tight. He'd carried me to the beach, to the far corner by the glass. Unless they'd been searching for us, no one would spot us tucked in the shadows, hidden behind the metal beams that supported the tanks.

Once my sobbing stopped, I sat quietly for a long while, waiting for the dam to burst back open. But I was hollow. I had no tears left to cry or pain left to tear me open. I'd gone numb, and I was grateful for it.

"Why"—I swallowed, trying to make my words come out more clearly—"why didn't you tell me?"

Alec loosened his hold on me, not much, just enough to give me the option of pushing him away. "I only heard yesterday. I reached out to Amery, trying to find out who'd—trying to get more information. I haven't heard back yet. I just didn't want to tell you until I knew if your mom was safe."

"He would have warned her, right?" I shifted enough to sit up on my own. "The second he found out, he would have made sure she hid."

"He would have done everything he could." Alec looked toward the glass.

"What does that mean?" I pulled away to kneel in front of him. "Alec?"

"They don't always tell the guards what's going on." Alec reached toward me, holding my waist like he wanted to steady me. "If they just gave the order to go in and raid the city without warning the guards what the Incorporation was planning in advance, he might not have had time to get to her."

"But you got to Mari and me. The night of the fire, you got us out."

"The plan to get you out was in the works long before the fire. We thought the attack on the dark corridor was going to ruin everything. We were really lucky we managed to get both of you out. Amery might have gotten lucky this time, too. We just have to wait for word."

"But Jaime. There's no way for me to find out about Jaime. He stays away from kep. Always has. He doesn't work in a factory. He's part of the fifty-seven percent." Fresh tears spilled down my cheeks. I didn't know where they'd come from. I'd been so sure I had nothing left.

"I can ask Amery."

"It's not worth it."

"If you love him, then it is." Alec pulled a perfectly pressed handkerchief from his pocket. "I can't imagine how hard it was for you to leave him like that."

"You really can't." I took Alec's handkerchief to dry my swollen face. "But if Jaime's still alive, he'll have gone so deep underground, Amery trying to find him would put Jaime in danger. He was dealing with vampires and weapons runners before I left. He stayed on the safe side of things because I needed him to. Without Mar and me to worry about, he'll be working with people who'd kill him for talking to a kep. I can't risk putting him in danger to make myself feel better."

"I'm sorry."

"It's not your problem."

"It's hurting you to not know where he is." Alec took my hand. "That makes it my problem. He was your boyfriend. He mattered to you. I—"

"Jaime was so much more than a stupid boyfriend or romance thing. He was the only one I could ever count on." I looked up through the glass. The domes on the slope above us glowed, reaching up toward the stars. "I love Mom and Mari. But Mom was always gone, and Mari's so little. Jaime was safe and solid. No matter what, he was there for me. He'd do anything to help me. He had my back. Always. Without question. Even if the whole world were on fire, Jaime would walk through the flames to get to me.

"And I just left him. I left him in a crumbling city, and now he's probably dead. He'd have done anything for me, and I abandoned him." I forced air past the pain in my throat. "I know I had to take care of Mari, but leaving Jaime was unforgiveable. I betrayed everything we had. I hate myself for it."

"I know you said you don't want Amery to try and find him. But after everything Jaime did for you and Mari, if Amery can help him, he will."

"And what deal would Jaime have to make?" I dried my face again and tucked the handkerchief into my pocket. I leaned closer to Alec, studying him in the shadows, trying to find something of the blood-soaked kep I'd believed him to be. "If Jaime's alive, he'd be better off not making deals with a kep."

"I don't think you understand the sort of man Amery is."

"What deal did you have to make with him to get you to protect Mari and me?"

Alec's face hardened, like a safety instinct had kicked in, telling him to lie to me. Or maybe to protect me. He closed his eyes and dragged his hands over his pale blond hair. "I'm helping you and Mari because I want to."

"You made a deal with Amery, and we both know it." I took Alec's hands. "I know Harper's bargain. What did Amery make you promise?"

"It's bigger than that." Alec looked down at our hands. "Amery raised me."

"What?"

"Since I was ten. My dad was an Outer Guard. Amery was his patrol partner. When Dad died, Amery took over raising me. Mom's still alive, but she never wanted kids. She only agreed to procreate to do her duty to the domes. She didn't get more interested in raising me once Dad was killed."

"Alec."

"I still lived with her. But I'd go to Amery's whenever I could. I ate there, did homework there. Slept on the floor when they'd let me get away with it."

"They?"

"Amery's married." He looked up, meeting my gaze. "He has a son, Wallace. He's only few months younger than you. I'd sleep in his room."

"I have a half-brother?" I pulled away from Alec. "Does my mom know?"

"Amery got married to protect her. There were rumors of him keeping a woman in the city. Starting a family in the domes seemed like the best way to keep your mother safe."

"Does Amery's wife know about Mari and me?" I dug my fingers into the sand. The grains weren't enough to stop my nails from digging into my palms.

"No. They have no idea he has another family."

Bile rose in my throat.

"They can't," Alec said. "It'd be too dangerous for you. One wrong word, and the domes could have killed you just to teach Amery a lesson."

"But Harper knows. You know." Everything started to tip again. "If he can't tell them, why would he tell you?"

"He didn't tell me until he needed my help protecting you."

"And you just went along with it? Do you hate Wallace and Amery's wife?"

"No." Alec knelt and took my shoulders. I didn't know if he was steadying me or restraining me. "But I understand that sometimes surviving inside the domes makes us do horrible things. I don't agree with Amery's lies. But I can't fault him for doing whatever it took to protect you and Mari. Amery is a good husband and father, even if the family he wanted to be with lived outside the glass."

"Then why didn't he leave?"

"How could he have helped you if he'd gone to live in the city? The Incorporation's rules force us to make impossible choices. He did the best he could. Every day, I try to be like Amery—choose the best option, no matter the cost."

"Is that why you helped Mari and me? Because it was the best option? You still haven't told me what deal you made with Amery. It must have been pretty awful if you tried to distract me by telling me he's spent the last seventeen years lying to his wife."

"It's complicated." Alec lifted his hands away from my shoulders and sat back in the sand.

"I have time."

"It'll be a lot harder for me to help you if you hate me."

"I'm locked inside glass with monsters who think murdering people like me is fun. Don't make me assume you're worse than them."

"I couldn't do it." Alec pressed his palms to the sand. "I couldn't handle being an Outer Guard for the Plains Domes. I always assumed it was what I wanted to do. Ever since I was a little kid. After my dad died, Amery worked it out so I could start training with some of the guards. Nothing formal, just something to distract me from grieving. Being an Outer Guard was everything I wanted. Until I actually went out into the city."

He started drawing in the sand. A square and some extra lines, like a weapon or a map.

"In training, they always say *combatants* or *workers*. They never actually call them *people*. Somehow, in my head, I never realized we would be fighting real people. That it would be my job to shoot mothers and children. And command would never tell me what the people had done wrong. They'd just tell me to shoot and expect me to pull the trigger."

He added to the drawing. More squares, more lines.

"My first night on duty in the city, we had to go after a Vamper nest. Five of them had started openly attacking people. It seemed clean cut. Blood suckers, bad. Stopping them, good. I was at the back of the formation. I never should have had to pull the trigger at all. But some regular humans got mad that our unit had stormed the building. Maybe they didn't understand why we were there. I don't know.

"They charged us from behind. I got the order. I had to shoot. I killed two men. They were barely older than me. They were so sick, they already looked like corpses. Then it was over, and we just got in the van and went home. We left their bodies in the hallway of the apartment building."

He drew a circle around the rest of the lines.

"I got so sick that night, I thought I'd never be able to eat again. I tried to hide it. Tried to convince myself I was just green. I'd get used to it. That I wasn't so broken I wouldn't be able to hack it as an Outer Guard. Amery saw straight through it. He came to me, and I told him everything. Told him I'd been an idiot to think I could kill people. The men I shot, they lived in that building. We'd brought violence into their home. They might have had kids in that building they thought they were defending."

He swiped his hand across the sand, destroying the image.

"Then why are you still a guard?"

He looked up at me, almost like he was shocked I'd actually stayed to listen.

"You can't just switch careers in the domes. Once you're an Outer Guard, that's it for life. The Incorporation has invested time and assets in your training. Those resources cannot be wasted. You serve, or you die. There is no way out. I thought I'd drown in the blood and death the domes had thrown me into. But Amery wasn't ready to give up on me." Tears glistened in Alec's eyes. "He figured out how to save me. The city by the Plains Domes, it's been on the edge of destruction for years. Violence is expected. There's no way out of it. Amery arranged my transfer to the Arc Domes."

"Why here? Because of Mar and me?"

"Because there isn't a city here. At least, not like at home. The city that serves the Arc Domes is through the mountain. There are miles of tunnel between us and them. We don't live under constant threat of attack."

"Our city was never a threat to the Plains Domes."

"You outnumbered us. The Council made sure none of us ever forgot it. I can feel the difference in the air here. The sense of security. Even after the explosion in the medical corridor, there isn't any fear."

"Has it occurred to you that the Council here might just be stupid?"

"It's a lot deeper than that. The city through the mountain, it's not like the one back home. The Incorporation designed it. Clean manufacturing. Self-sustaining food distribution. An allotment of medical care."

"That sounds like the domes."

"They're not inside glass, they're not as protected. But the city through the mountain was built to survive. What the guards from the Plains Domes are being made to do, that will never happen here. I will never have that sort of blood on my conscience." He stretched his hands out in the sand, reaching toward me. "When

Amery secured my transfer, I asked him if there was anything I could do to repay him for saving me. He told me about you and Mari. He asked me to help him get you out. Your father is the best man I have ever known. There's no way I could refuse to help him."

"It's nice that you don't have to feel guilty, but your leaving didn't stop any of the people in the city back home from dying. It just put the gun in someone else's hand."

"I know. I've gone through it a hundred times, trying to figure out if I'm less guilty of their deaths because I'm not there or if I'm just a coward who ran."

"Could you have stopped it? Could you have saved any of them?"

Alec stared out at the waves. Their steady lapping calmed me, even though I knew how much their creation had cost.

"All I could've done is gotten myself killed, and it wouldn't have made a damn difference." A tear rolled down his cheek. "I never could have saved anyone."

"Then you did the right thing. You helped Mari and me. You got us out of the city. You saved us at the depot." My hand moved forward until my fingers brushed against his. I don't know if I'd wanted to touch him or if some instinct had told me that keeping him near me would be the closest thing to safety I could find. "It might not be the difference you wanted to make, but you kept my little sister alive. That counts for something."

"I'm sorry I couldn't do more." He took my hand.

"Don't." I leaned forward, brushing away the track the tear had left on his cheek. "Don't add more weight to your shoulders that doesn't need to be there."

"Thank you, Lanni." He wiped the tears from my cheeks and brushed my tear-wet hair away from my face. "I promise I will keep protecting you and Mari. And I'll find out everything I can from Amery. And I'll...I'll do what I can to make things better."

His hand was still by my cheek.

I leaned into his palm. "I believe you."

I looked into his emerald-green eyes, and everything in the world went quiet. The waves stopped rustling, and the final ringing of the scream in my head fell silent.

I leaned forward, just an inch, just enough to shatter the safety of the space between us.

He shifted his hand, grazing the side of my neck, as he brushed his lips against mine.

My breath caught in my chest as I willed him to hold me and give me something to forget the horrors of the world.

He kissed me again.

My heart raced as he wrapped his arm around my waist, drawing me toward him.

The world melted, and warmth ran through my body. I pulled myself closer to him, wanting more. Needing to dive so deep I never had to remember anything else existed.

I gasped as his fingers found bare skin at my hip.

He kissed me one more time before easing himself away from me, leaving just enough space between us that our bodies couldn't touch. He rested his forehead against mine, keeping his fingers tangled in my hair.

"I should go," he said.

"Don't."

"You had an awful night. You're upset."

"Then keep kissing me."

He brushed his lips against mine so gently it was like a ghost of the kiss I craved.

"I won't take advantage of you, Lanni." He pulled away from me and sat back in the sand. "Even if I'd never promised Amery anything. I still couldn't."

"Nobility. How inconvenient."

"Will you be okay if I leave you here?"

"You stay." I stood and brushed the sand off my pants. "Mari's probably already asleep at Miranda's. I'll have to carry her home."

"Do you need help?"

"I've got it. She hasn't grown that much yet." I made myself smile for him. "See you around, Alec."

He caught my hand with a gentle touch. The tips of his fingers grazed my palm, sending tingles cascading up my arm. "We don't have to wait to run into each other. You could let me know if you have time. If you want to see me, I'll be there."

I kissed the top of his head. I couldn't think of anything to say, so I just walked away, leaving him on a beach that never should have existed.

CHAPTER TWENTY-TWO

I tried to stop reality from crashing back down around me as I walked toward Bloom Dome. But without Alec to distract me, I couldn't keep the grief from pushing its way back into my chest.

I'd known the moment I got in the truck to come to the Arcadia Domes I would never see Mom or Jaime again. But knowing they were out there in the world had somehow made it seem less definitive and hopeless. Even though I'd never see them or talk to them again, I hadn't felt so utterly alone.

I pulled Alec's handkerchief back out of my pocket, brushing away a fresh round of tears. I needed to look calm for Mari. I couldn't let her guess why I needed to hold her so tight.

My legs ached like I'd just run for hours as I climbed the steps to Bloom Dome. I wondered if my muscles had given into despair, if my body wanted me to slide back under the waves to drown in grief.

"Dammit, Alec." I wanted to be in his arms again. I wanted him to make me forget again.

The lights had already been turned low along the path to Miranda's house. I'd been out too long. She'd want an explanation.

I wondered if telling her I'd been with a boy would cause elation or punishment.

I stopped at the fountain and splashed water onto my face, washing away the last traces of my tears.

Maybe that's what I could tell Miranda. The dance hadn't gone well and I'd run off to cry in the shadows because Gideon had abandoned me in the crowd.

It seemed like a good story, a drama worthy of a girl who'd only ever known the safety of the domes. Even Gideon might believe it.

I shoved aside the tendril of guilt that wriggled in my stomach.

"The world is ending, Lanni. Who you kiss doesn't rank in the top thousand problems. Get your shit together."

I shook out my shoulders and looked toward Miranda's house. Five minutes of conversation with our guardian and I'd be able to go home.

A weird light flickering beside the path caught my eye. The glow brightened as it rose.

I ran toward the light. It wasn't even two hundred feet down the path.

A single-unit house hid back in the trees. Flames flickered through the first-floor windows.

"Shit." I bolted toward the house. "Fire! You have to get out, there's a fire." I banged on the door. "Get out, there's a fire!" I grabbed the doorknob. The heat of it stung my skin, but it wouldn't turn. "You have to get out!"

I stayed silent for a moment, listening for voices over the crackle of the flames.

I couldn't hear anyone, but it didn't make sense. Whoever lived inside should be home and asleep.

"Shit." I sprinted back toward the fountain. "Someone get help, there's a fire!" I shouted as loudly as I could, hoping someone would hear and actually do something.

I jumped into the fountain, dunking myself in the water to soak my clothes. My boots squished as I scrambled over the side and ran back toward the house.

I pulled Alec's now-sopping handkerchief from my pocket and tied it around my face. The familiar feel of fabric covering my nose and mouth dulled the edges of my fear as I kicked the door of the house.

Pain throbbed up my leg, but the door didn't budge. "Just break." I kicked again. Something inside the door cracked.

"Fuck you." The door gave on the third kick, swinging into the house.

I took a deep breath before running inside.

Heat bit my arms through the thin layer of my wet shirt.

"Hello!" I shouted over the crackling roar of the flames. "You have to get out!"

A chair in the kitchen had been knocked over. A glass and a plate had been smashed on the floor, but there wasn't a person in sight.

I choked on the smoke leaking through the handkerchief as I turned the corner toward the living room.

No one. Not a thing out of place. The flames had consumed the sofa and climbed the walls.

Steam rose from my clothes as I ran up the stairs to the bedrooms.

I grabbed the knob of the first door I reached. It was hot, but not enough to burn. I tried to twist it, but it wouldn't move.

"There's a fire, you have to get out." I coughed the words.

I kicked the door, breaking through in two tries.

A kid lay on the bed. He was young. Maybe ten. There was blood on his chest. So much blood.

"Oh no, no, no." I stumbled toward him and pressed my fingers to his neck. He was already dead. Someone had closed his eyes. Someone with blood on their hands. They'd left two red streaks on his eyelids.

I swallowed the sour in my throat and ran to the other room. That door had been locked, too. I kicked it open. A man lay on the bed. A woman lay on the floor. Blood covered both of their torsos.

I choked on the smoke as I went to the man. He was dead. They hadn't bothered to close his eyes. The woman had more cuts on her. Like whoever had killed her had allowed her to fight back. But then they'd stabbed her lower stomach over and over. Slicing between her hips like they'd wanted to tear out her womb.

I shoved myself to my feet. The smoke had gotten too thick for me to see the door. I dropped back down and crawled out of the room.

I couldn't tell if the sounds of the fire had changed or if it was only my own blood roaring in my ears as I went back down the stairs.

The blaze had climbed the walls. I gagged on the tainted air as I tried to remember which way I'd entered the house.

An ear-splitting crack sounded above me, and chunks of the ceiling fell, sending a swarm of sparks raining down on me. I closed my eyes and turned my face away, letting my palms take the sting of the burning.

"Why aren't the sprinklers working?" The frightened shout barely carried over the blaze's roar.

I headed toward the sound.

Pain scorched my right leg. I didn't stop to look down.

I could see it in front of me, an opening in the wall of fire.

Bracing for more pain, I charged forward, letting the flames lap at my skin as I burst through the blaze and into the open air beyond.

There were screams. Lots of screams.

Someone grabbed me, knocking me to the ground and smacking the place where my right leg hurt.

I started to scream at the pain tearing through my leg, but I didn't have enough air. I ripped the handkerchief off my face and hacked the smoke out of my lungs.

"We need to put out the fire!"

"The guards are on their way."

"Why isn't the alarm going off?"

I pushed myself to my knees. My whole body shook as I tried to get enough air past my coughs to speak.

"They're dead." My lungs protested even those two words. I dug my nails into the ruined flowerbed and demanded my body do more. "Someone killed them. They're all dead."

CHAPTER TWENTY-THREE

I never thought to wonder if there was more than one kind of monster lurking inside the domes. But the shadows here have different shapes.

Some seem like they could have been normal if they'd been born outside the protection of the glass. If they'd been like me and lost their parents before they could talk. If they'd grown up in the boys' home, hiding in the basement as often as they could, choosing the darkness over risking the wrath of the older boys. If they had led my life, they might have ended up right where I am now.

But there are others who were born shrouded in evil. It's not the Incorporation that drove it into their souls. They entered this world as demons with human skin.

They want to hurt the people outside the glass, not for any purpose beyond the thrill of watching blood flow. If they can't kill outside the glass, they will infest their own home with violence.

But the most depraved of the monsters I've seen trapped in these walls are the ones who would never think of touching a weapon. They delight in inflicting the most inhumane torture on the people who should be their neighbors, and they don't see the evil in their actions. They call it duty. They think they are leading the domes toward a better future. They cannot *see the human cost of their grand plans, even as they watch the people they should care for suffer.*

There are moments when I wonder if we should try and save those who were born with souls that do not crave suffering. Even though they were born inside the glass, they could be like us, I'm nearly certain of it.

But they've been tainted by the Incorporation. They've lost the ability to see us as human. Even if we could try to teach them the truth we fight for, the risk would be too great.

We cannot endanger our cause in an attempt to save those who would happily sit by while we are slaughtered.

When the bloodshed begins, we will all be painted with the same red as we fight our way to freedom. The contents of a man's soul will not change the truth of our enemies' sins.

But I needed to write it down. I needed even this fleeting record that I had seen the difference between the monsters and had cared enough to wonder if any of them could be saved.

Even the best among them would never have spared a thought to wonder about saving me.

See you in the embers,

~C

CHAPTER TWENTY-FOUR

My head hurt.

Somehow, with all the tubes attached to my arm, gooey patches stuck to my skin, and medicine I'd breathed in through the mask strapped to my face, none of it had gotten rid of the pain in my head.

The bright white light of my hospital room jabbed into my eyes as they changed out the goo on my leg. The doctor hadn't let me look at my burned flesh as they cut my pants away. I'd wanted to tell her seeing my burn wouldn't be as bad as seeing that dead family, but my lungs hadn't been working well enough to speak.

They'd covered most of my body in the cool gooey patches, leaving only strips of fabric to maintain my modesty. Like I had the energy to care about who saw my nipples.

There was a murderer in the domes. Someone had gone into that house, stabbed that family, then risked the lives of everyone in Bloom Dome by setting a fire to cover their tracks.

A few dead kep didn't matter to me, but having a killer on the loose who didn't mind stabbing kids did.

I had to get to Mari. I had to keep her safe. I had to find out who'd murdered that little boy, and if I couldn't stop them, then I had to get Mari out of the domes and away from the killer. And I didn't give a shit if I had to walk through the domes completely naked if it would help me protect Mari.

I wanted to run home and take care of her. But even I was smart enough to know I was too injured to be able to make it up the stairs, let alone defend my sister.

So I lay very still, not fussing as they peeled away bits of my damaged flesh and applied thin patches to help my skin grow back, while I tried to ignore the pain in my head that kept getting worse with every passing minute.

Low voices rumbled in the hall. Sometimes, they'd get louder, like whoever prowled outside my door had gotten angry. Then the voices would change, and they'd get quiet again.

They must have given me something to dull my senses because time seemed to bend a little. Maybe I fell asleep, but it felt like I'd just blinked and it had taken me a second to force my eyes back open. But someone had removed the breathing mask, and I couldn't remember anyone touching me.

The temptation to rip the tubes from my arm and go find Mari made my headache worse. I shifted my hand, trying to reach across my stomach to pull the tubes from my other arm.

A wave of nausea and pain rolled through my body.

The computer started beeping. The sound dug into the top of my skull.

"Stop it." My voice came out gravelly. "PAM, stop it."

A doctor ran through the swinging door.

I caught a glimpse of black-uniformed guards lurking in the hall.

"Miss Roberts, you're awake." The doctor's voice stayed steady even as her fingers flew over the computer screen.

"Make the noise stop," I said.

"Of course."

The beeping stopped, but the little flashing light in the corner of the screen kept going.

"When can I leave?" I asked.

"Let's worry about patching you up first," the doctor said.

"When can I go home?" I gritted my teeth against the pain and pushed myself up onto my elbows. "I need to get to my sister."

"Miss Roberts, you need to lie down." The doctor placed a hand behind my back. "You sustained burns over thirty percent of your body and a fair amount of lung damage."

"I don't care about my lungs. I care about my sister." I tried to push the doctor away from me and gasped as pain ripped through my side like I'd torn part of my healing flesh.

"Lie down now, or I will sedate you." The doctor held my gaze.

"Then you need to bring my sister to me." I lay back down on the bed. "She needs to be here where I can watch her."

"It's been discussed with your guardian." The doctor examined the patch on my side where the ripping pain had come from. She made a sound somewhere between a tsk and a growl before opening the metal cabinet on the wall and pulling down another sealed package of the goo-covered sheets. "It was decided that Mari should wait to visit until you've had some time to heal."

"I'm fine. Bring Mari here."

"Your sister is a child. She doesn't need to see you like this."

"She'll be fine."

"Maybe you don't understand the extent of your wounds."

"No. You don't understand Mari."

I watched as the doctor peeled away the bandage on my side. A raw, red patch of skin bigger than my hand had split down the middle. Ooze leaked from the wound.

"Mari would want to watch so she'd know how to put a burn bandage on by herself." I focused on the ceiling, imagining my sister's face instead of letting myself wonder how bad my leg must be to have needed more treatment than my side. "She tried to do a tourniquet on a woman's arm when the depot exploded. That was a little too much for her, so she helped pull the glass out of my side instead."

"She sounds like me when I was little. When the kids in my class got hurt screwing around in the practical lessons, I always wanted to see the wounds before they were taken to medical. I wanted to know how bodies worked and how to make people better. And maybe you're right. Maybe your sister would be fine. But your guardian wants her kept away until we can dress you in a hospital gown. So let's focus on getting you there quickly, okay?"

"How long do you think that'll take?" I closed my eyes, like relaxing might somehow make my skin regrow faster.

"If you hold very still and don't try to fight me on your treatment, we should be able to get you into a gown in a few hours."

"Then I need to see Guard Alec Quinn. He can go to Mari. He'll make sure she's safe."

Cold ran up my arm as the doctor shoved some new medicine into my veins.

"Your sister is with your guardian. She's perfectly safe."

"Someone murdered three people and set their house on fire. If I hadn't run into that fire, the killer might have gotten away with making it look like an accident."

"What?" The doctor stepped away from me.

It hadn't occurred to me that word wouldn't have spread.

"A kid was stabbed and left to bleed out. I can't let that happen to Mari. The killer, the way they ripped through that woman's gut, it looked personal. If I had been mad enough at someone to slaughter their whole family and light their house on fire, and then some random teenager had come along and fucked the whole thing up"—hot tears ran down my cheeks. I wanted to wipe them away but couldn't move my arms—"I don't think I'd just forget the whole thing and move on. I'd want to hurt the person who'd ruined my plan."

"There are guards in the hall that want to talk to you. If you're up to it, I can let them in. If there's any danger—"

"Then Guard Quinn needs to be with my sister. If the ke—guards will send Alec to Mari, I'll talk to them."

"Right." The doctor's hands shook as she touched a few more buttons on the computer screen. "Of course."

I shut my eyes as she went out into the hall to talk to the guards.

The voices got loud again.

Then the doctor's voice disappeared and it became a one-way conversation, like one of the guards was talking into the com on their wrist and the responses were too soft for me to hear.

A few minutes later, the doors swung open again as Captain Pace and a woman in a guard's uniform came in.

"Miss Roberts." Pace gave me a nod. "I'm glad you're awake enough to talk."

"I won't talk to you until I know Guard Alec Quinn is with my sister," I said.

"The doctor gave us your request," Pace said. "I've sent word for Guard Quinn to go to your guardian's home."

"Let me know when he gets there." I closed my eyes.

"Miss Roberts," the woman said, "if what you told the doctor is true, then we need to speak to you immediately."

"I've seen Alec run," I said. "He's pretty fast."

"Miss Roberts," Pace said, "I don't think you've met Captain Tate. She is the head of the Dome Guard. Alec is one of my men, he's an Outer Guard, and as his captain, you have my assurance that he is protecting your sister."

"Then call him." I kept my eyes closed, hiding the panic I knew they'd betray.

"Miss Roberts—"

"I found three murdered people and almost burned to death. I will wait until I know my sister is safe."

"Guard Quinn, this is Captain Pace."

I opened my eyes.

Pace spoke into the black band around his wrist.

"Yes, Captain Pace." Alec's voice came from the band.

"Miss Roberts would like to confirm you are with her sister," Pace said.

"Just arrived, sir. Tell Miss Roberts I have Mari. She's a little tired, but she's fine."

More tears burned their way down my temples.

"Thank you," I said.

Pace tapped his com band.

"Now tell us what happened." Captain Tate stepped closer to my bed.

I pressed my palms to the white sheets below me.

"I got back to Bloom Dome and went to get my sister from our guardian. I saw that the house was on fire. I tried calling for help, but no one came, so I kicked through the door to see if there was anybody trapped inside. There were three people upstairs. All of them had been stabbed. The kid was still in his bedroom. The man was killed on his bed, but it looked like the woman had fought back. The other two had only been stabbed once, but the woman's lower stomach had been torn apart, like someone was trying to gut her.

"None of them were alive, so I went back downstairs to try and get out. I think that's when my leg caught on fire. By the time I got out of the house, there were other people outside. I told them what had happened before I passed out."

"What were you doing out so late at night?" Tate's lips tensed like she was trying not to glower at me.

"I..." I didn't know if I could tell them about Alec and the beach. I didn't know if I'd get him in trouble. I didn't know if I'd get in trouble with Pace for kissing Alec when I was supposed to be at a dance with Pace's son. "I had a bit of a freak out at the dance. I'm still not the best at dealing with everything that happened at the depot. I went to the beach for a while to calm down. I don't even know how long I spent there, but when I left, I headed to get my little sister."

"Do you often wander through the domes at night?" Tate asked.

"Sometimes," I said. "I don't sleep well. It's easier for me to wander than to risk keeping my sister awake. She's just a kid. She needs her rest."

"I spoke to the doctors," Tate said. "They were surprised you weren't worse off after running into a burning building. Your injuries should have been more severe."

"Are you mad I'm not crispier?" I asked.

Pace rocked back on his heels.

"I'm just trying to understand," Tate said.

"I jumped into the fountain before I went in," I said. "I soaked my clothes and the handkerchief I used to cover my face. It didn't save me, but if I should have been worse off, I'd guess it was that."

"Why did you jump into the fountain?" Pace narrowed his eyes at me.

"Because no one else was coming, and if I was going to run into a burning building, wet seemed better than dry. Why does it even matter? Someone killed three people. That person could be after me and my sister because I fucked up their plan to burn the bodies. Isn't that more important than why I tied a wet cloth over my face?"

"It absolutely is," Pace said. "Tate, these atrocities are happening inside the domes. I'm happy to assist in any way I can, but as you are the Captain of the Dome Guard, this incident clearly falls under your jurisdiction. I only have one more question for Miss Roberts. Why Guard Quinn to protect your sister?"

"Because I don't know who the people in that house were or why someone would plant a bomb in the medical corridor." I let out a shuddering breath. It didn't stop more tears from spilling over. "I don't know who I'm supposed to trust. But Alec saved Mari at the depot. He carried her out after the explosions when I couldn't even find her. I know he'll protect her."

"Good enough." Pace looked to Tate. "Unless there's anything else you need from me, I'll be out of your way."

"I'll keep you updated." Tate watched Pace leave and didn't speak again until the door stopped swinging behind him. "Now start over from the beginning."

"What beginning?"

"When did you first notice the fire?"

"Why does that matter?" I looked toward the door, willing the doctor to come back with something to ease the growing pain in my leg.

"Three people were just murdered inside my domes. Everything matters."

CHAPTER TWENTY-FIVE

"It's not fair that Miranda wouldn't let me see you." Mari perched beside me on my hospital bed, clinging to my arm that wasn't attached to a bunch of tubes. "I told her it didn't matter if you were burned, I should be with you. And she said it was too scary for a child. And I wanted to tell her I was brave and had seen plenty of bad things and I didn't get scared, but I couldn't think of how to say it without her getting suspicious, so I cried instead like Harper told us to, but then she made me stay with her for hours while you were in here, but I swear I wanted to come as soon as she woke me up and told me you'd almost burned to death."

"She didn't say it like that, did she?" I wanted to hug Mari as much for my comfort as for hers. They'd propped me up in bed to greet her so I could almost reach, but since I was still covered in gooey patches, I settled for squeezing her hand.

"No. Miranda said there'd been a fire and you tried to help and ended up with *grave injuries*, which means almost burned to death." Mari curled up close to my side, leaving an inch between her and my rapidly healing skin.

"Careful." Alec stepped forward from his place by the door.

"She's okay," I said. "Having Mari close is the best medicine in the world."

"I told Miranda that, too," Mari said. "She's nice and good at braiding hair, but she's not good at listening to me."

"She doesn't know how brave you are," Alec said. "You're not an average seven-year-old, Mari."

"But I'm not allowed to tell her that." Tears rolled down Mari's cheeks. "And she wouldn't let me be here. And if something is bad enough for you to send Alec to watch me, then we should be together."

"You're right, we should. But you were safe with Miranda, and that's what matters."

"Safe from what?" Mari sat up, furrowing her brow as she stared into my eyes. I knew that look. She was searching me for lies. "Miranda's our guardian. Why did Alec need to come watch me, too?"

I didn't let my gaze flick toward Alec as he inched closer to my bed.

"The fire wasn't an accident. Someone killed the family in that house and then set the fire. If someone wants to murder people, I need to make sure they don't have a chance to get anywhere near you."

Mari frowned. "The people who died in Bloom Dome got murdered?"

"They were stabbed," I said.

"But the announcement said they died in a tragic accident," Mari said. "There's a memorial, and they're going to review fire safety for everybody."

"What?" I looked to Alec.

"I don't know if this is the time." He nodded toward Mari.

"Don't be like Miranda." Mari spoke through gritted teeth.

"Everything that's come through the com has said it was an accident." Alec stood right beside my bed, keeping his voice low like he was afraid of being overheard. "Did you tell Pace and Tate?"

"Of course I did. Why would they lie about what happened? Everyone in the Arc Domes is in danger."

Alec scrubbed his hands over his hair. "I don't know. They've got to have a reason. Maybe they're keeping the investigation quiet so they can trap the killer."

"Or they're gambling with people's lives in a stupid attempt to not cause a panic." I held Alec's gaze. We'd finally gotten to something I couldn't say in front of Mari. "If they're not willing to admit there's a murderer on the loose, I can't trust them to protect Mari."

"I'm going to have to report back to the barracks eventually," Alec said. "If I refuse, they'll toss me in a cell and I won't be able help anyone."

"I won't be allowed out of here until at least tomorrow." I looked up at the ceiling.

"I'll stay here and protect Lanni," Mari said. "I'm little, but I'm fast."

"The doctors won't let you stay here," Alec said. "Twenty-minute visit, that's what we're allowed. She needs rest."

"I'm fine," I said.

"You almost died, Lanni," Alec said. "You're not fine. And pushing too hard isn't going to help anybody."

"I—" My lungs stung. I couldn't even take a deep enough breath to argue with him. "Mari, this hall is guarded. It has been since the bombing. I'll be safe in here, and Alec will watch you at Miranda's. We're going to be okay."

Mari leaned in so I could kiss the top of her head without having to move. "Why would somebody want to kill those people? There's no reason to fight. Everybody has everything here."

"I don't know, Mar. But the Dome Guard will figure it out, and everything will be okay."

"Time for us to go." Miranda popped her head through the door.

"We just got here." Mari clung to my hand. "I don't want to leave Lanni."

"The memorial service for the Kain family starts soon," Miranda said. "Your sister tried to save their lives. It's only right you should represent her while we remember them. Lanni is a hero."

"Come here," I said.

Mari leaned in so I could kiss her head one more time. "Stay close to Alec, and don't worry about me. I'll be okay."

"I love you." Mari kissed my forehead and scrambled backward off the bed.

"We should clean you up before the service." Miranda smoothed Mari's collar.

"Can you wait outside for one second while I talk to Alec?" I asked.

Miranda glanced between Alec and me. "Sure."

I gave Mari one more smile as she followed Miranda into the hall.

"Are you actually okay?" Alec asked as soon as the door closed behind them.

"No. Everything hurts like hell, and I'm worried about Mar."

"I'll take care of her." Alec gently touched my hand.

I laced my fingers through his, grateful to have something tangible to hang onto that didn't make the world spin even further from my control. "Can you get a message to Walsh, ask him to come here?"

"Sure. But if there's something else I can do, just tell me."

"If you get sent back to the barracks before I'm out of here, I want him to watch Mari."

"You don't trust the guards?" Alec glanced toward the doors.

"No. I've never trusted kep, and after what I saw last night, I know they can't even be trusted to not kill their own kind."

"I'm a kep."

"Don't rub it in and make me start doubting you. I really need to not doubt you." I took a breath, letting pain push away the panic surging in my chest.

"Lanni, last night…I don't regret any of it." He looked down at our joined hands. "But if I hadn't taken you to the beach, you would have been home with Mari. You wouldn't have been the one to find the fire."

"Don't." I gripped his hand. "I'll be fine. And if you hadn't taken me away from the dance, I might have stabbed someone and gotten kicked out of the domes."

"I could have taken you home instead of to the Salt Dome."

"I'm glad you didn't."

"Me too." He bent down and kissed the back of my hand. "Did you tell Pace and Tate where you were before you found the fire?"

"I told them I was at the beach, but I made it sound like I was alone. I didn't know if you'd get in trouble."

"I'm barely out of school. I'm eighteen. No one would have a problem with us being together." Alec sat on the edge of my bed.

"Except Gideon. I was supposed to be his date. I slipped out on Captain Pace's son."

Alec stayed silent. I couldn't read his face.

"You don't have to say you don't care what your captain thinks." I slid my hand away from his.

"I don't want to make life harder for either of us." Alec glanced toward the door again. "You're in Captain Pace's training program. He's on the Domes Council. Having someone like him on your side is an asset. You can't afford to alienate yourself."

"It's fine." I wished I could stand up and leave, or do anything besides lie in a bed where I could barely move my hands I was so covered in bandages. "Just take care of Mari for me."

"We don't have to walk away from this. Tell Gideon you're sorry about the dance. Don't go out with him again. Let him down gently. We'll wait two weeks before letting anyone see us together. As long as Captain Pace doesn't think you ditched Gideon for me, we'll be fine. Lanni, I"—he touched my cheek—"I want to spend more time with you. But I have to keep you safe."

"And that'll be easier with a captain who isn't pissed at me for ditching his son."

"Yeah."

I turned my head enough to kiss his palm. "Go. Take care of Mari."

"Rest." He brushed his lips against mine.

I shut my eyes tight, trying to find a bit of the blissful distraction the beach had offered. But he walked away, leaving me stuck in a hospital room.

Penned in. Trapped.

There were three metal cabinets along the wall. Two of them had locks.

There were six panels of lights on the ceiling.

One computer monitor.

One door.

Three tubes in my arm.

I wanted to count the patches they'd put on my skin, but they'd draped a sheet over my legs and I couldn't see them anymore.

"Fuck."

I closed my eyes, trying to will myself to sleep, but Mari had gone to a memorial service and someone in the domes liked to plant bombs. If they wanted to do maximum damage, targeting a gathering where most of the kep would be packed together in one place...they wouldn't get a better chance.

"Shit. Shit."

My foot started to jiggle. Pain shot up my leg.

"Fucker."

I focused on breathing, inhaling as deeply as I could without hurting my lungs.

You've never been good at sitting still, Jaime's voice whispered in my head.

"We never had time to sit still," I whispered back. "We were too busy trying to survive."

You have to heal to survive. Let your body do the work.

"I can't. I can't sit still. I don't want to have this much time to miss you."

I waited for Jaime to say something back. Something comforting and wise. But he stayed silent.

My breath shook in my chest, sending pain into my lungs.

I gripped the sheets on my bed, trying to anchor myself to something beyond grief. I couldn't let myself feel what losing Jaime really meant. That hurt would send me tumbling into a dark and horrible place I wasn't sure I was strong enough to climb out of.

A rumble of voices came from the hall. The tone of the murmured words seemed somber, but then a man laughed like someone had told a great joke.

I opened my eyes at a knock on the door.

"Come in." I tried to sit up straight. A throb of pain in my back quickly reminded me I couldn't.

"Thank you so much." Walsh entered the room, still talking to the guards outside. "I'll keep it short."

"Alec talked to you already?" I asked as Walsh held his hand to the door to keep it from swinging back open.

"Alec? No." Walsh listened at the door for a moment before coming closer to my bed.

"He's been guarding Mari for me. If they send him back to the barracks, will you watch her? I know it can't be official since you're not a guard."

"So the fire was intentional." Walsh looked at the ceiling. "I managed to catch a whisper about a stabbing—"

"For the last time, yes. Should I write up notes on how I found three corpses and hand them out to everyone who visits me?"

"Not in a good mood?"

"I can't move. What do you think?"

"May I?" Walsh reached for the sheet that covered my legs.

"If you want to see a bunch of nasty goo, go for it."

He flipped the sheet back, whistling at all the patches on my legs. Most of the skin looked normal through the goo, but my right leg was still bright red with uneven growth where they'd cut away the unsalvageable tissue.

"Humans and fire don't go well together." Walsh gently draped the sheet back over me.

"I actually noticed that when I was running through the burning building."

"Better you than me." Walsh perched beside me. "There's no way I could hide my *differences* with those kinds of burns."

"Thank you for the comfort."

"I've never been one for comfort."

"Then why are you here?"

"To make sure you were actually alive. To see if what I'd overheard was true."

"I thought they were pretending the Kains' deaths were an accident."

"They are. But eavesdropping is one of my talents." Walsh winked.

"Well, I hope you're good at covering your tracks. Add one weird death to three murders and Tate is going to be sniffing around everywhere."

"Sniffing?" Walsh said. "Are you making a dog joke?"

"No. I'm trying to make sure you don't do anything stupid."

"I'm not going to do anything stupid. I've already checked item number two off my list. Now I have to play the waiting game."

"Why?" I reached forward, ignoring the pain ripping through my arm as I grabbed Walsh's wrist. "What was number two?"

"Don't worry about it."

"Did you kill the Kains?" I whispered, like that was the only thing we'd said that could expose us.

"I'm not an idiot." Walsh laid his hand over mine. "I'm nowhere near done with my work here. Going around stabbing people would cause questions I need to avoid. But someone's gone murder-happy, and they're making my work harder."

"Then we have to stop them. Listen in, sneak around, do whatever it takes to find out who's doing this."

"One dead kid, and you're suddenly worried about Incorporation lives."

"One attack in the dome where Mari and I live, and I want the fucker found before they come near my sister. I saw what the killer did to those people. I screwed up their plan to hide what they'd done. If there is even the slightest chance they could be pissed enough to try and come after me, I have to make sure they don't have any opportunity to hurt Mari." I loosened my grip on Walsh's wrist, letting my hand slide down to hold his. "I helped you, Walsh. Help me with this."

Walsh looked up, staring at the fourth of the six lighting panels. "I'll figure out what I can. But no promises. It could be something as random as a jealous lover."

"And you'll watch Mari."

"Like an animal stalking prey."

I laughed just enough to start coughing.

"Careful there. I'm witty, but I'm not worth lung damage."

"You're right, you're not."

Knock. Knock.

Both of us froze.

"Lanni, can I come in?" Gideon called through the crack in the door.

"Shit," I whispered.

"So the dance went well?"

"Not even a little." I pulled away from Walsh. "Come in."

"Lanni, I brought th—" Gideon stepped through the door like

he was falling in line to report for duty. His gaze flicked from me to Walsh and back again. "Sorry. The guards didn't…I didn't mean to interrupt."

"You're fine," Walsh said. "I just stopped by for a quick visit. After everything Lanni went through last night, I thought she might want to see a familiar face."

"Right." Gideon stepped a little farther into the room.

"Weird though," Walsh said, "as long as I've known Lanni, she's never actually run into a burning building before."

"She behaved incredibly bravely," Gideon said.

"She can also hear and speak," I said.

"Sorry." Walsh squeezed my hand. "Hospitals make me uncomfortable."

"You go. I'll be fine here. Just check in on Mari for me?" I said.

"I'll make sure all the talk of your heroics doesn't freak her out," Walsh said.

"Thanks."

He bent down and kissed the back of my hand, then smiled and gave Gideon a nod before leaving.

"I really didn't know he was in here," Gideon said.

"Don't worry about it." I made myself smile. The effort was exhausting.

"I just wanted to make sure you were okay." He had none of his usual bounce as he crossed to my bed. "And I brought you this."

He laid a piece of blue paper next to my hand. He'd folded it into the shape of a flower, but something about the shade of blue lit a flare of loathing in my gut.

"Thanks." I touched the flower, too wary of moving to actually pick it up.

"It's something I read about. Bringing people flowers in the hospital. We're not allowed to pick the flowers in the domes, but I figured a paper one was better than nothing."

"It's nice."

"I snagged the paper from my dad. That's not really allowed either, but I figure they won't miss one sheet from the massive stacks of pamphlets they give the outsiders."

"Right." I eased my fingers away from the blue. I'd read so many of the kep pamphlets. I wondered what propaganda would have been printed on the page. I wanted to burn it.

Gideon didn't seem to notice.

"Look, I know it's selfish of me to come in here after all you went through yesterday." The words tumbled out of him. "You almost died, and I shouldn't be taking up your time with lame excuses. But I just really needed to say that I'm sorry for last night. I never should have left you alone like that. Really, I never should have brought you anywhere near my brothers, but with them storming off, I just stopped thinking for a minute. You were my date, and my place was with you."

"It's fine."

"No, it's not. You stood up to my brothers. Talking about what happened to you at the depot can't be easy."

"It's fine." I lifted my hand enough to reach for his. "Really."

"Good." Gideon gave a nod that somehow involved his whole body. He looked to the door. "I also—and it feels stupid to ask while you're recovering—but you and Walsh, is that, I mean if you'd rather I leave, I can."

"What?" I squinted at him, focusing on his face, trying to make sure I hadn't somehow fallen asleep and missed the part of his question that made it make sense.

"I heard some people talking before about how you and Walsh were a couple. And if I misread anything, I'm sorry."

"I..."

It was a perfect out. I could say I was interested in Walsh. Walsh could pretend to dump me. I'd be free from Mrs. Hale's meddling, and I might even be able to steal some more blissful distraction with Alec.

But having Captain Pace pissed at Walsh would be worse than him being mad at Alec.

"I'm not interested in Walsh," I said. "Not in a dating sort of way. It's nice to have him around. To have someone who understands where I'm from. But I think we know too much about each other to ever go beyond close friends."

"Oh." Gideon rocked back on his heels. "That's nice. I mean, I don't want to read anything into that, but I'm glad you have a friend here."

"Me, too. And I'm glad I have a tour guide who knows all the best hiding spots in the domes. I only got to see the willow tree. When they finally let me out of here, I wouldn't mind seeing some of the other stops on the tour."

"Good. That's good." Gideon started doing his excited bounce. "The doctors here are the best the Incorporation has to offer. They'll get you patched up in no time. I guess I should let you rest now. So you can leave sooner." He took a hesitant step toward me, then bent over and kissed my cheek. "Do you mind if I visit you again?"

"With any luck, I'll be out of here before you have time."

I wasn't that lucky.

CHAPTER TWENTY-SIX

It took three days for them to finally let me out of the hospital.

Between the awful glare of the white lights, trying not to think about Jaime and Mom, and spending every second Mari wasn't with me panicking about if she was all right, it felt like I was going to explode any minute.

Walsh couldn't find out anything about the investigation, neither could Alec.

When they called Alec back to the barracks, the panic and constant mind-itch of not knowing what was going on outside my room got bad enough I would have gladly drunk Harper's nasty wine to dull my worry. But since she never came to visit, I didn't have a chance to beg her for any.

Things didn't get better when Miranda showed up to fuss over whether or not I was actually ready to leave.

I sat on my bed, still stuck in my hospital gown, listening to the doctor and Miranda bickering in the hall. I knew I should be grateful to have someone who cared enough to harass the doctor about my health, but I wanted to break out of the hospital so badly I would have chewed my leg off like an animal stuck in a trap if I'd thought it would give me a shot at breaking free.

"It doesn't matter if it's unpleasant. It's your job." Miranda's words carried through the door. "Someone's got to tell her."

"Tell me what?" I called.

The voices in the hall fell silent.

I watched the door, waiting to see which of them would be brave enough to come into the room first.

Miranda popped her head in. "Are you all right, Lanni?"

"I guess that depends on what neither of you wants to tell me," I said.

"It's nothing," Miranda said in a voice that was too chipper, even for her. "The doctors have done an excellent job fixing all the damage from the fire."

"Then can someone give me pants so I can leave?" I asked.

"Sure." Miranda ducked back into the hall for a moment before finally stepping all the way into my room. "Clothes are on their way."

"Look, whatever it is, can you just tell me?" I stood up, tensing the muscles in my neck to make sure I didn't wince at the ache that shot up my legs. "I'm not glass. I won't break."

"Of course not," Miranda said. "You are such a brave girl, and it just seems a pity the doctors couldn't help you more."

"You just said I'm fine."

"You are." Miranda bustled across the room and untied the string at the end of my braid. "But unfortunately, burn treatments can't regrow hair."

"What's wrong with my hair?" I shook my braid out for the first time since I'd been in the hospital. It felt strange. Too light in my hands.

"Quite a bit of your hair was burned." Miranda steered me toward the computer screen in the wall. "The doctor suggests leaving it long and just wearing it back all the time, but I didn't think it was fair to send you home and have you realize the extent of the damage when you tried to shower."

She tapped the screen, turning it into a mirror.

The ends of my hair had been singed. Swatches had been burned entirely away. The patchy layers reached all the way up above my shoulders.

"Honestly, if you hadn't been so quick-thinking and wet your hair before going into that house, there would be a lot more damage." Miranda met my gaze in the computer screen. "And it will grow back."

"It doesn't matter." I ran my fingers through my hair. Strands crumpled and fell to the ground. "It's just hair. Does the doctor have scissors?"

"I brought some." Miranda pulled a pair from her pocket.

"You came prepared to chop off my hair?"

"I just didn't want you to go through this alone." Miranda rolled a chair over from the corner. "I know you're older, so I really don't have as much work to do with you as I do with Mari, but big changes after a trauma can be hard. I know you're strong, you've had to be, but I didn't like the idea of you taking scissors to your own hair."

"I wouldn't have." I sat down. "I'd have let Mari do it. She'd think it was fun."

"I used to cut my daughter's hair all the time." Miranda tipped my chin up and adjusted my shoulders. "This should turn out better than trusting a seven-year-old. How short?"

"Whatever you think is best."

"All right."

I shut my eyes, ignoring the feeling of the scissors touching the back of my neck. I tried to think of something to say so the sound of my hair being chopped wouldn't seem so loud.

"How old is your daughter?" I never would have asked a question like that in the city. Too many people died young. Unless you could see somebody's kid with your own eyes, it was better not to mention they'd ever existed.

"She's twenty-two now and about to make me a grandmother."

"Congratulations."

Miranda brushed my hair off my shoulders. "Thank you. I'm excited to have a tiny one to take care of again. I hate having an empty house. That's why I volunteered to be a guardian for you and Mari."

"Will you stay Mari's guardian, once you have a grandbaby to tend to?" I gripped the sides of the chair as the scissors came around to cut just under my chin.

"Of course. I wouldn't abandon Mari or you. You girls have been through so much. The last thing I'd want is to cause you any more heartache."

"Thanks."

I fell silent as she worked her way around to the other side of my head.

The weight of my hair falling away made me feel exposed—naked in a way I hadn't known was possible.

"There are still a few places where you can see it was burned." Miranda brushed off my shoulders for the fourth time. "But once it grows in a bit, we'll give it a fresh cut."

"I'm sure it's great."

Miranda tapped the computer again, pulling the mirror function back up.

It's just hair. It doesn't matter.

I stood up and stepped in front of the screen. The girl the computer showed me looked nothing like the girl I'd been my whole life.

Even after the burns and days spent stuck in the hospital, I had better color in my cheeks than I'd ever had back home. My face had filled out, too, softening the once-familiar angles. There were no bags under my eyes. And my hair barely went past my chin.

I reached up and touched the ends.

"You don't like it?" Miranda said. "We could always go for something a little edgier like your friend Harper."

"It's not that. It's just…my mom always insisted I keep my hair long. My whole life. And now it's just…gone." Tears burned in my eyes.

"I'm so sorry, Lanni." Miranda hugged me. Like an actual, maternal hug.

I couldn't even remember the last time I'd hugged Mom. I'd been so mad at her toward the end.

"She may have liked your hair long," Miranda said, "but I think she would have loved the courageous young woman you showed yourself to be. She would be so proud of you, no matter how short your hair."

"Thanks." I eased away from Miranda. I didn't manage to wipe away my tears before she saw them.

"I'll run out and check on your clothes, and then we'll get you home."

"It's still the school day."

"You don't have to go." Miranda hesitated by the door. "You should head home and rest."

"I've spent days staring at the ceiling in here. The last thing I want is to go home and stare at the ceiling there."

"If you're sure." Miranda gave me an understanding smile, like she knew I couldn't face the threat of having more time to think, and disappeared into the hall.

I tried to listen to what she was saying to the doctor, or guard, or whoever else was lurking outside my room, but all I could hear was the low rumbling of their voices.

I ran my fingers through my hair and brushed more of the cuttings off my neck.

"It's not a big deal." I tucked my hair behind my ears. The ends tickled my chin. "It doesn't matter at all."

Saying it out loud didn't make it feel any more convincing.

She wanted it long so I could fit in with the kep. Mission accom-plished. Let it go.

I waited for Jaime's voice to reply, but the hidden corners of my mind couldn't come up with anything comforting for him to say.

But I could still picture him trying to hide his smile as he shook his head at me, judging me for worrying about something so small when there were life or death matters I actually needed to focus on.

"Thanks, Jaime."

Miranda brought me a whole new set of clothes, complete with brand new boots. As I tied the still-stiff laces, I couldn't help wondering if Mr. Lewis's calculations had accounted for boots being ruined by house fires.

I begged my way out of Miranda walking me to class, but the doctor insisted on having one of my two door guards follow me.

I waited until we got a few corridors away before speaking to the man keeping three feet behind my shoulder. "I know how to get to class. You really don't need to walk me."

"I have orders, miss." The guard stayed in step right behind me.

"Are you going to wait outside my class to walk me home?" I asked.

"My orders haven't gone that far yet."

"Are you following me because there might be a murderer who wants to kill me?"

"I'm just following orders, miss."

"Great." I resisted the urge to sprint to class just to be rid of my guard faster. I felt decent for having almost died, but I didn't want to push too hard and end up on another gurney.

I slowed down even more when we neared my classroom.

"Could you do me a favor and stop following me before my classmates can see you?" I asked. "I don't want to sound ungrateful, but the last thing I need is people paying extra attention to me because a guard walked me to class."

"I'll stop at the stairwell," the guard said.

"Thanks." I ran my hands around my neck one more time, getting rid of as much of the stray hair as I could, before walking up the steps and into class.

I kept my chin tucked as I headed toward my desk, like I was trying to sneak in after running late dropping Mari off.

But Mrs. Hale said, "Lanni!" and then someone started clapping, and someone else started stomping their feet. The whole room cheered as I sank into my seat.

I wanted to melt into the floor, or even better, threaten all their lives if they didn't stop.

But my gaze drifted to Walsh, and he widened his eyes at me while giving a tiny bow with his head.

"Thanks." I forced a little smile onto my face. "I'm happy to be back."

Gideon reached out and took my hand. He twined his fingers through mine. Just for a moment. Just long enough to make sure everyone saw it wasn't a simple handshake.

"Your hair looks great." He let go and sat back in his seat.

"All right, all right." Mrs. Hale hushed the class. "We still have a lot of material to get through before the end of the day. Gideon, perhaps you can help Lanni catch up on the work she missed."

"I'd love to." Gideon grinned, and I realized I would have been better off staring at the ceiling in my room.

CHAPTER TWENTY-SEVEN

"I like it at Miranda's." Mari bounced on her butt on her bed. "She has a much bigger house than we have here, and she knows all sorts of nice things to make with the food rations she gets."

"Thanks, Mar." I dug in my closet, trying to figure out which of my shirts fit the loosest.

"Are you telling me Lanni isn't a good cook?" Walsh said.

I turned around and threw a shirt at him. "I'm a fine cook."

"I help with the cooking," Mari said. "And Miranda taught me how to make some new things."

"Will I get to taste any of these delights?" Walsh furrowed his brow.

I could tell he was trying not to laugh at Mari, but she didn't seem to notice.

"Are you staying for dinner?" Her bouncing got bigger.

"He's going to be hanging out in here with us for a while." I found my cherry-red shirt.

"Why?" Mari tipped her head to the side.

"Because the guards still aren't publicly admitting there's a murderer on the loose, and I want an extra set of hands keeping you safe," I said.

Anyone else in the domes would have glared at me for saying something like that to a kid, but Walsh didn't flinch.

"Is Alec on duty?" Mari bounced off her bed and went to the kitchen.

"Until tomorrow morning," I said.

"Then I'll make food for the three of us," Mari said. "And maybe Harper. Should I go get Harper?"

"I don't know." I stepped into the bathroom, carefully ignoring my reflection in the mirror as I changed my shirt. "I can walk you down the hall if you want to try."

"I can take her," Walsh said.

"Thanks." The red shirt had the same soft, new feeling as the rest of the tops the domes had issued me. I tucked my hand under the seam near my waist. Plenty of room.

I waited until the door to the hall closed to snatch a washcloth from our stack of clean laundry and slip back into our room. I darted to the kitchen like I was a thief in my own home.

There were only three knives in the kitchen drawer, and these blades weren't made for slicing human flesh. Normal citizens weren't allowed to have weapons in the domes.

Didn't matter in the end. Three people had been killed. Probably by a knife identical to one in my drawer.

The smallest knife was tiny enough I wasn't sure I could do much damage with it. The largest might've given me an advantage in a fight, but it was bigger than the weapon I'd carried back home. I grabbed the medium knife and wrapped the blade in the washcloth.

I tucked the whole thing in my waistband by my hip.

A weird sense of relief flooded through me, like I'd just regained the use of my hands.

I slid the kitchen drawer shut as the hall door opened.

"We only have two chairs, so Walsh and I can sit on the floor."

Mari dragged Harper into our room. "I would say Lanni and I could sit on the floor, but she almost died."

"And I'm the shit who didn't visit her." Harper raised her jug of homemade wine to me. "Sorry for being a shit. I'm glad you're alive."

"Don't worry about it." I backed away from the door to let the three of them in. "You weren't obligated to come see me covered in nasty burn goo."

"I got to go see her." Mari pushed Harper and Walsh to sit on her bed then dragged a chair over to the kitchen. "And Alec and Walsh went to see her."

"So I'm a super shit." Harper took a drink straight from her jug.

"I'll grab you a cup," I said.

"It's okay." Mari climbed on top of the chair to reach the pots above the stove. "You can be a part of things now."

I ducked around Mari to pull down a cup.

"Get one for you, too," Harper said. "Walsh, want some illicit homemade wine?"

"Not this time," Walsh said. "I'm on *guard the hero* duty."

"The family was murdered." Mari set the pot on the stove and scrambled backward off the chair. "Lanni's afraid of us being murdered, too. So I got to spend lots of time with Alec, and now Walsh is going to watch me. Murderer on the loose isn't the best, but I get to spend more time with people. I like that part."

"Way to look on the bright side, Mar." I handed Harper her cup.

"Dr. Kain was murdered?" Harper poured herself some pink wine.

"Every time you tell people, someone else gets to be surprised." Mari pulled our grain bin from the drawer. "That's a good part, too."

"Fuck." Harper downed half her cup. "Fuckity fuck fucks."

"What?" I sat between her and Walsh.

"I've been so grateful she was dead, it never occurred to me someone might have had the guts to actually kill her."

"Why would you be grateful she was dead?" I asked.

"Because the woman was evil and had to go," Harper said.

"I poked around," Walsh said. "Nothing about Dr. Kain screamed *evil*."

"Everything pointed straight to *savior*." Harper refilled her cup and passed it to me.

"And?" I took a sip of the pink wine. The sweetness of it stung my teeth.

"There's nothing the Incorporation loves more than making grand sacrifices to preserve the human race," Harper said.

"Which sacrifice was Dr. Kain willing to make?" I took another sip. It didn't taste any better. I passed Harper back her cup.

"I'll tell you later." Harper nodded toward Mari, who was happily chopping vegetables while still standing on a chair.

"She's fine," I said.

"She shouldn't have to be." Harper set the jug and cup down on the table and stood, like she needed to be ready to bolt out of the room. "Kain wrote a paper for the Incorporation. A detailed analysis of the genetic issues that could come from allowing Incorporation citizens to choose their own breeding patterns for the next three hundred years."

"But people don't choose their own breeding patterns," Walsh said. "There are very strict limits on how many children can be born."

"It's not just about the number." Harper dug her fingers into her cropped hair. "It's the pairings. Basically, Kain concluded locking people inside glass and limiting the gene pool is a terrible idea."

"It's a little late to change that now," I said.

"But the damage can be limited by assigning breeding partners based on a thorough genetic analysis," Harper said.

"What?" I gripped the blankets on the bed.

"Everybody gets a genetic screening, and the doctors choose who you're supposed to breed with. Like we're no better than farm animals. Just lock us in a pasture and don't let us out until we've managed to make a genetically preferable baby. Oh, but it gets worse. In Kain's perfect world, genetic variation would be best maintained by creating mostly half-siblings. So not only do the doctors tell you who to fuck, they get to pass you around."

Bile rose in my throat. "They won't do that here. Her paper must have been rejected. Mrs. Hale is obsessed with getting me to date. She wants me to find a boyfriend. That means I'm supposed to make the choice."

"For now." Harper's hand shook as she picked up her wine. "In the Plains Domes, there were whispers about Kain's breeding plan being used in some of the other locations, rumors about really horrible things happening in the River Domes before they fell. I don't know anything for sure, but it's enough to make you want to kill your liver."

"No one would ever agree to go along with it," I said. "I can't—there's no way that could happen."

Walsh laid his hand on mine. "I'd never let it happen."

"You two are so cute thinking they'd give anyone a choice," Harper said.

"Why didn't any of this come up when I was looking into Dr. Kain?" Walsh said.

"You were probably looking for bad things in her life," Harper said. "That paper was just another one of her many accomplishments as she worked for the good of the Incorporation."

"That feels like motive for murder." I squeezed Walsh's hand before pulling away. "But not enough to kill her husband and son."

"The partner she chose and the kid she wanted?" Harper downed the rest of her glass. "She planned to steal those decisions from all of us. I'm not saying I agree with murder, but that kind of vengeance makes sense to me."

"But that means we're okay, right?" Mari asked.

I looked toward her. I'd forgotten she was there.

"I mean, if she wrote a paper that made people mad, then the person who killed her won't come after us." Tears sparkled in Mari's eyes. "And now that she's dead, they won't do what her paper said. Cause I wanted to work with the animals, but I don't want them to treat me like one. I don't want to be like—"

Mari froze, staring wide-eyed at Walsh.

She doesn't know he's like us.

"I'm sorry, Mar." I stood up and crossed the few steps to the kitchen to lift her off the chair. "You're so grownup, I forget what things you shouldn't hear."

"I'm glad I heard." Mari wrapped her legs around me, letting me hold her on my hip like I used to when she was smaller. "You're my sister, and it's my job to protect you. I can't do that if I don't know what we have to be scared of."

"We don't have to be scared of anything." I pressed my cheek to the top of Mari's head as I shifted my weight back and forth, rocking her. "A dead woman had a very cruel idea. She's gone. We're here, and there's no way I'd ever let anybody hurt you. You got that, Mar?"

"I got it." Mari held me extra tight. "I have to get down, or dinner will burn."

"Okay." I set her back on her chair by the stove.

She wiped her face on her sleeve before going back to working on the vegetables like nothing was wrong.

A gnawing guilt twisted in my stomach. I should have been more careful to shield her from the horrible truth of what the Incorporation would even consider doing to its precious citizens.

But she'd heard worse, far worse, before. And if anything happened to me and I wasn't around to protect her anymore, Mari would need to know the truth in order to protect herself.

"We're going to have to narrow it down a lot," Walsh said. "There's no way to know how many people that paper pissed off."

"The explosion in the medical corridor," I said, "what got ruined?"

"I think you'd need a security clearance to find that out," Harper said.

"Great." I dragged my fingers through my hair. A weird shock ricocheted through my chest as they reached the bottom of my hair far too soon.

"We'll figure it out," Walsh said. "And in the meantime, I'll be here to watch out for you."

"And I'll be here to drink." Harper raised her glass.

"Thank you. Both of you," I said.

"Dinner's almost ready." Mari climbed down off the chair.

"I'll set the table." I grabbed our four allotted plates from the cupboard. I trailed my fingers over their smooth surface, trying to remind myself to be grateful.

I had the closest thing to friends I could hope for under the circumstances. I hadn't burned to death.

I cut around Mari toward the table.

Someone knocked on the door. I spun toward the sound, letting go of the plates as I reached toward the knife hidden at my hip.

Walsh dove in front of me, catching the plates before they hit the ground.

"I got it." Mari reached for the doorknob.

"Don't open it!" I shouted.

Mari looked back at me with a frown.

"I'll get it." Walsh set the thankfully unbroken plates on the table. He picked Mari up, setting her behind him before opening the door.

I could see the tension in his shoulders as he turned the door-knob, like a coiled-up spring ready to snap.

Or a predator.

"Oh, umm, hi," Gideon said from the hall. "Is Lanni here?"

"Yeah." Walsh stayed frozen for a second before stepping out of the way.

Ignoring the scuffling sounds behind me, I squeezed around Mari and to the door.

"Hi." I made myself smile for him. "Sorry, I wasn't expecting you. It's a little chaotic here."

"Yeah." Gideon's gaze flicked to Walsh. "I just wanted to stop by and make sure you were okay."

"Everybody's here to make sure I'm okay." I raised an eyebrow.

"Do you want dinner?" Mari peeked around me. "Lanni and I can share a plate."

"I've already eaten," Gideon said. "I just wanted to see if you felt up to a walk, but I don't want to interrupt."

"You're not interrupting," Walsh said. "Harper and I can watch Mari if Lanni wants a breather."

"Breather from what?" Mari asked.

Walsh put a hand on my back, pushing just hard enough for me to be sure he really wanted me to go.

"I didn't invite you over here to be babysitters," I said.

"I don't need a babysitter." Mari frowned.

"Harper and I are pretty great," Walsh said, "but with all the stress you've been under, some time with Pace might be exactly what you need."

Walsh smiled as he spoke, staring right into my eyes like he was drilling his message into my brain.

"A little peace and quiet might do you some good," Gideon said.

"As long as there are no hospital room lights." I turned around to kiss Mari on the head.

Harper leaned against my closet door. Her jug had disappeared, but I didn't think she was only chewing her lips out of fear of the captain's son catching her with illicit wine.

"I'll see you all later." I let Gideon take my hand as we walked down the hall.

CHAPTER TWENTY-EIGHT

I'd like to think someone wanted me once. I hope my parents felt an ounce of joy when they found out I was on the way.

I hope they were smart enough to feel panic and guilt, too. This is not a world children should be born into.

Our world is full of pain, want, and blood. What hope could I ever have had for a peaceful life?

But if I hadn't been born, I wouldn't be here to fight. And how many more would have suffered if I hadn't agreed to face the monsters that torment us?

I am glad I was born into the ruins of the world. If I had been born to parents who gave me a life inside the glass, I never could have forgiven their selfishness.

Every time I discover more about the monsters of the Incorporation, I realize how far they have strayed from what humanity should hope to be. They weaponize what should be beautiful and defile the very act of creating life.

How is there not an uprising every day? How do parents allow the system to continue, knowing what will be expected of their children?

I still don't know where this path will lead us and what order we hope to create. I can't see a solution that leads to a better world and not just *giving a new face to the ones who hide from the pain those on the outside suffer.*

But I am more certain than ever that any future we bring will be better than the hell the Incorporation has sold to its citizens as paradise.

Some of them will even be grateful for my work as they burn. I pity them.

See you in the embers,

-C

The leaves rustled as something scurried through the shadows a few feet away from me. I shut my eyes, trying to convince myself not to run from whatever small animal made the noise.

The creatures in the Tropics Dome weren't like the disease-infested rodents in the city. If they could've harmed the kep, they'd have been locked safely away.

Gideon lay beside me, deep in the canopy of trees, farther back than they'd ever allowed our class to go. The weird grasses surrounded us, and the trees grew so close together, I couldn't see the glass above me.

"It's almost like we're outside." Gideon rolled toward me, propping himself up on his elbow.

"If things like this existed outside, we wouldn't be in here."

"No, we wouldn't." He touched my hand. Not grabbing onto it, just laying his fingers on top of mine. "You know, you don't have to be okay."

"What do you mean?" I reached back to move my hair so I could turn to face him. My fingers grazed my bare neck. I shoved away the odd grief that pressed on my chest.

"I mean, you can be honest with me." He brushed my hair away from my face. "You don't have to pretend you aren't freaked out about what happened to the Kains. You can talk to me about what happened at the depot. I don't just want to take you to dances, Lanni. I want to be a part of your life. And that means being there for you when things are hard."

"Did you get sent on another elder visit to get that advice?"

"Nope. Figured it out on my own."

"I didn't know you were smart." I lay down facing him. The handle of my kitchen knife pressed into my hipbone.

"I'm top of the class." He lowered himself down so his face was only a few inches away from mine. "Had to make sure I had something going for me in case I never outgrew runt status."

"If I ever need help with my schoolwork, I'll know who to ask."

"I'll help you with whatever you need." A palpable, terrified energy radiated off him as he laid his hand on my waist.

"What I really need is to understand why all of this happened." I rested my hand on his chest. "And the Dome Guard are so determined to keep it quiet. I almost died. How am I supposed to go back to normal if I don't even know why I nearly burned to death?"

"I'm so sorry." He rubbed his hand along my back.

I slid forward, resting my head against his shoulder. "Dr. Kain's papers, the way she wanted to control breeding in the domes—"

Gideon tensed.

"It scares me. It should terrify all of us. But there are a lot of steps between fear and killing." I shivered despite the warmth of the rainforest.

He held me closer.

"I need to know what the bomb in the medical corridor was meant to destroy." I tipped my chin up to meet his gaze, my lips hovering an inch below his. "I feel like if I could understand that, maybe the whole thing would make sense, and I'd be able to breathe again."

"I want to help you." He lowered his hand to the small of my back.

"Can you ask your mom? She's a doctor, she must know. Or maybe your dad?" I slid my hand up to his cheek, arching my back a tiny bit with the movement, just enough to make sure he noticed my chest pressing against his. "Please, I don't know who else I can ask."

"I'll find out. I promise."

"Soon?" I let hope sneak into my voice.

"Soon."

I lifted my head and brushed my lips against his cheek. I took my time laying my head back down, letting my mouth hover a breath away from his. "Thank you, Gideon."

He closed the gap between us, kissing me.

I held him close as he explored my lips, allowing him a moment to revel in his daring before teasing his lips with my tongue. I sighed as I laced my fingers through his hair, shifting my hips to make sure he couldn't feel the handle of my knife as I pulled myself close enough that he couldn't hide any of the ridges of his body.

He gasped and pulled away from me, blushing hard enough I could see his skin darken even in the dim light.

"Sorry." I lay on my back, biting my bottom lip in a poor attempt to hide my smile.

"No, don't be...I mean—I should go talk to my mom before she falls asleep for the night." He sat up, brushing the dirt from his shoulder.

"You'll tell me what she says tomorrow." I knelt in front of him.

"Yeah. Yeah of course."

"Thank you." I gave him one more, slow kiss. "You're my hero."

CHAPTER THIRTY

The lights had been turned down for the night by the time I made it back to Bloom Dome. Everything looked the same as it had the night of the fire. I didn't need to go to Miranda's to pick Mari up, so I just took the path straight home. Still, I kept looking for damage along the way. But the deaths of three people hadn't left a single blemish on the Incorporation's demanded perfection.

I hated it.

A sick feeling boiled in my stomach as I got closer to our home. I rubbed my hand across my mouth, like I could somehow wipe away any trace I'd ever kissed Gideon.

You're not her. You aren't Mom.

I stopped in the corridor of our building, pressing my forehead to our door.

Gideon would bring me the information I needed. As simple as that. And since I had the opportunity to find out what the bomb's target had been without drawing suspicion or hurting anyone, I really couldn't question if I'd done the right thing.

Knowing that didn't make the awful feeling in my gut go away.

I shook out my shoulders, hitched a smile onto my face, and opened the door.

Our room was dark.

Panic jolted through me. I grabbed the knife on my hip and reached to turn on the lights at the same time.

"Leave them off." A shadow moved at the back of the room. "I just got Mari to go to sleep."

"Walsh?" I slipped inside, shutting the door behind me.

"Mari almost passed out standing up, so I sent Harper home and made Mari go to bed." Walsh edged around the table to meet me in the tiny area that was our kitchen.

"Thanks."

"Not a problem. I'm going to be spending the night here anyway, and I'm good with kids."

"Really?"

"Grew up surrounded by them."

"Still, thanks." I ran my fingers through my too-short hair.

"So how did it go?"

"I'll find out tomorrow." I peeked around him to see Mari's shadow as she peacefully slept. "I really have no right to ask you to stay here."

"I thought we were getting to be friends."

I raised an eyebrow. It somehow surprised me that Walsh could see the small movement in the dark, even though I knew what he was.

"Comfortable allies then." Walsh shrugged. "It would be wrong for me to abandon you when you and Mari could be in danger. Besides, you're not the only one who needs to know who the hell decided starting a fire was a good way to hide murder, and I think Gideon is a lot less likely to want to help me than you. Making sure you don't get killed isn't just the right thing to do. It's also in my best interest."

"In that case, you can have my bed." I sat in a chair to unlace my boots.

"I'll be fine. I don't need to sleep."

"Ever?" I froze.

"I can go a few days without. I slept last time Alec was watching her."

"No wonder you had time to stalk me. You could spend all night doing homework." I pulled off my boots.

"It's convenient, but it can get a little weird when one day just goes straight into the next."

"Never thought of it that way." I pulled the knife from my hip and tucked it under the top edge of Mari's mattress. "Take my bed anyway. You can lie down and pretend to be normal."

"I'm really fine."

"Mari and I shared a bed until we got here. And if the killer comes, I'd rather not have to cross a room to get to her."

"I can keep you safe." Walsh sat on my bed.

"Is it dumb if I almost believe you?" I lifted Mari's blankets just enough to climb in behind her.

"I'll never lie to you, Lanni," Walsh said. "I may not be able to tell you everything you want to know, but I won't lie."

Mari turned over, snuggling into my arms like she had back home. I kissed her on the head and fell asleep before I could think through why guilt was still gnawing at my stomach.

CHAPTER THIRTY-ONE

"Lanni."

I tried to pull myself out of the depths of sleep.

"Lanni." A warm hand touched my shoulder. "Lanni, if you don't want anyone to see me leaving, I should go now."

I opened my eyes to find Walsh kneeling beside the bed.

"What time is it?" I whispered.

"Too damn early." Walsh grinned. "I'll get into the trees and keep watching from there. I just didn't want you to wake up to find me gone."

"Thanks." I eased my arm out from under Mari's head.

"Do you want me to conveniently bump into you to walk to school together, or just creep behind?"

"Be a creeper. Gideon said he'd bring me information this morning. I don't want you to scare him off."

"Smart." Walsh went to the window as I slipped out of bed, trying not to wake Mari.

He pushed the window open and planted his hand on the sill, like even though the window was chest-height, he was just going to hop up and through.

"How fast can you run?" I asked.

"Faster than you."

"I mean it." I touched his arm. The warmth of his skin felt nice, like I could curl up against him and drift back to sleep.

"I've never accurately timed myself. Below a two-minute mile? Faster when sprinting?"

"Fast enough to get to us if something goes wrong?"

Walsh brushed his fingers across my cheek. "And with a bad enough temper to live up to the werewolf name if someone tries to hurt you or Mari."

"See you in class." I lifted my hand away from his arm.

He jumped through the window.

I didn't even hear him land outside. I slid the window closed, got my knife back out from under Mari's mattress, and went to sit on my own bed.

Walsh hadn't gotten under the sheets. Or, if he had, he'd perfectly remade the bed.

I curled up against the wall, watching Mari sleep, trying not to think.

There was so much I should be getting done and so many memories I needed to avoid.

I wasn't a detective or a guard. I had no business prying into why someone had killed Dr. Kain. If I'd found out about something dangerous like that in the city, I would've just avoided the mess until things calmed down. But there was no way to skirt around anything in the domes.

Paradise is just a pretty cage.

I closed my eyes, trying to picture Jaime, pretending Alec had never told me about what the Plains Domes had done.

Even if I figure out why the Kains were killed, how am I supposed to find out who did it? I pictured myself saying to Jaime.

He lifted his arm, letting me nestle close to him. He flicked the ends of my short hair until I nudged him in the stomach with my elbow.

Please, I thought. *Jaime, help me.*

He sighed. *Do you even want to find the person who did it? If they want to kill kep and destroy kep property, let them. You don't have to stop them. You just have to make sure they don't hurt you and Mar.*

Tears rolled down my cheeks.

How am I supposed to do that? I pressed my cheek to his chest, wondering how I could find his scent so comforting when I didn't even have the words to properly describe it. Something like the streets after a heavy rain.

Find out why they did it and make them think you're on their side. Jaime tightened his arms around me. *You don't have to be a hero, Lanni. You just have to survive and take care of Mar.*

Tears caught in my throat. I tried to swallow the sound. *We were supposed to take care of her together.*

I know.

My chest started to shake as I lost the battle against grief.

"It's okay."

A much smaller hand than Jaime's took mine.

The bed shifted as Mari crawled up next to me. She knelt beside me and wrapped her arms around my shoulders.

"We'll be okay, Lanni." She kissed my cheek. "As long as we're together, everything will be okay."

"I love you, Mar." I picked her up and set her in my lap.

"I love you, too. What's the matter?"

"Just homesick."

"I get homesick, too." Mari looked up at me. "I know things are better here, but I still miss it there."

"And that's okay."

"But you know something I don't ever miss about home?" Mari grinned.

"What?"

"Breakfast slop." She stuck out her tongue and giggled. "I'll make us breakfast."

She wriggled off my lap.

"I'm supposed to do the cooking, Mar."

"I like cooking." Mari dragged a chair to the kitchen. "Maybe I could get a job cooking workday lunches for people when I grow up."

"I think you'd be really good at that."

By the time I'd washed my face well enough to look like someone who'd actually slept and eaten the grain cakes Mari had made, we'd managed to dawdle long enough for it to be time to go to school.

She'd gone back to her usual bouncing self, half-skipping, half-jumping down the paths as she told me everything she hoped she'd get to do in school.

I wondered if Gideon had been a bouncy kid, too. Like a rabbit always ready to run from his predator brothers, or if the bounce had come from excitement when he'd grown big enough to defend himself. Even thinking about Gideon made the weird guilt creep back into my stomach.

"We're going to get to plant actual plants." Mari tugged on my hand. "We don't get to choose what kind we're going to plant, but we get to touch the seeds and everything." She shivered with delight.

"I can't wait for you to tell me how it went at the end of the day."

"You'll come meet me?" Mari stopped and looked up at me. "I like Miranda and Alec, but it feels best when you come get me."

"A horde of vampires couldn't stop me." I bopped her nose and herded her down the hall, letting my wrist graze the handle of the knife I'd hidden at my hip.

Gideon came into sight around the arc of the corridor, leaning against the wall, clutching his tablet to his chest like he didn't know what to do with his hands.

"Lanni." He smiled when he caught sight of me, but the smile didn't reach his eyes. "Mari." He gave her a nod that turned into a bow.

Mari snickered.

"Can I walk you to class?" he asked.

"Sure," I said. "I have to take Mari to her room first."

"Absolutely." Gideon took my hand, clutching it like someone might drag me away. "You should. Let's head on over. Tardy for school is a bad start to the day."

"Okay." Mari wrinkled her nose at Gideon. "But I think maybe you should try to sleep more. You don't look so good."

"I'll take that into consideration." Gideon gave another smile that looked more like a wince.

He kept his pace quick, almost dragging me along behind him as I tried to balance not dropping my tablet and making sure Mari kept up.

"When does your dad want to restart the training program?" I asked.

"Day after tomorrow," Gideon said. "No offense to you, but I was surprised they stopped it at all. I think the choice came from the Council, though Dad would never admit to being told what to do."

"Why did they stop training?" Mari ran to walk backward in front of us.

"Reassessment of priorities," Gideon said.

"Huh?"

"Here you go, Mar." I pulled my hand from Gideon's to grab her shoulder before she could back past her own classroom. "I can't wait to hear all about the seeds when we get home."

"You'll be here to get me?" Mari bounced on her toes.

"I'll be here." I kissed the top of her head and shooed her up the stairs.

"You do more mothering with her than either of my parents ever did with me," Gideon said.

"She's my little sister. It's my job to take care of her."

"It's a lot more than that, even if you don't see it." He took my elbow, leading me down the hall.

"Want to tell me why you're freaking out?" I whispered, jogging to match his pace.

"Not in the hall." He cut up a set of stairs and into a classroom that didn't have any desks in it. He closed the door before looking around the empty room, like he was trying to find someone hiding in the non-existent shadows.

"What did your mom say?" I asked.

"Nothing." Gideon shook his head and checked the corners again. "She said it was nothing for me to worry about. Totally blew me off."

"Shit." I looked toward the stairs, wondering if Walsh was listening. "There's got to be another way to find out."

"Oh, there is." Gideon stepped close to me to whisper. "Whatever was destroyed, there'd have to be a log of it and some kind of communication between doctors, right? I know my mom's password, so I waited until she was asleep and logged onto her workstation in our house."

"What did you find out?"

"Bad things, really freaking bad things." Gideon gnawed on his lips.

"Well, tell me." I took his arm. "Whatever it is, it'll be a hell of a lot better than not knowing."

"They destroyed the DNA bank."

"What?"

"The"—pink rose in his cheeks—"the DNA bank. I don't think they have them in the other domes. The Arc Domes have a higher medical research capacity than any of the other locations."

"Whose DNA were they researching?"

"They weren't, not like that." The pink in his face darkened. "The DNA bank had...samples from all the adults in the domes. Preserved in case there was ever a disaster in the Arc Domes that left an unsustainable gene pool."

"Unsustainable how?"

"An illness, a recessive trait causing a hereditary disease, an incident leading to mass infertility. With such a small genetic pool to begin with, the doctors didn't want to take any chances. Procreation has to be maintained, so they collected the samples"—the deep crimson climbed to his forehead—"from all the adults to keep frozen. Then if something horrible happened, they could use the saved DNA to refresh the gene pool."

"And have women carry the children of men who died a hundred years ago." My stomach disappeared like someone had scooped away all the organs I needed to survive.

"Or the child of a woman who died a hundred years ago. The bank held both *types* of samples."

The red in Gideon's face didn't seem entertaining anymore.

"And someone destroyed all of it?"

"The bomb was placed on that cooling unit." Gideon took hold of my elbow like I'd been swaying. Maybe I had. "Dr. Kain was in charge of the project."

"She wrote that paper, about wanting to control who could breed with who. Talking about people mating like we're no better than livestock."

"I wanted to think you were wrong," Gideon said. "I wanted to think you'd been traumatized and were seeing connections that didn't exist. But it all fits together too well."

"Someone wanted to stop Dr. Kain's work. It could be anybody. It should be everybody."

"They'd have to be desperate to resort to murder, Lanni. They must know they'll be caught eventually. If they're just trying to do damage on their way out, I don't think you're safe."

"I already know that." I yanked my arm away from him and started to pace.

"The Dome Guard will have made the connection. There's no way they could've missed it."

"Then why are they lying about the Kains' deaths?"

"Either because they don't want to cause a panic, or because they're afraid too many people will agree with the killer."

"They can't just do nothing." I froze, looking toward the stairs, wondering if I should call for Walsh so someone with experience in plotting to kill people could offer some insight.

"Lanni, I'm scared for you." Gideon took my hand.

"How secure is your position in the Arc Domes?"

"How do you mean?"

"I'm new here. I punched someone. I only have a little rope to work with. But you're the captain's son. If you cause a little trouble, will they hurt you?"

"What kind of trouble?" The color drained from Gideon's face.

"The good kind." I kissed his cheek. "The kind that keeps me alive."

CHAPTER THIRTY-TWO

*M*oths are drawn to flames. Wolves are drawn to blood.

It's the simple facts of nature that control us all, no matter how logical we strive to be.

Humans are drawn to disaster, wanting to know what horrors they managed to escape. They want to watch their enemies burn. Watching their allies crumble can bring an even more primal form of glee.

If mankind had managed to move beyond such horrible delights, I wonder if we might have survived. If watching others thrive had been as good a pastime as watching them fail, could we have avoided the wars that slaughtered so many?

I don't think a core trait of compassion being bred into humans would have prevented all the disasters that plague the earth. Greed ruined the environment, hubris allowed disease to flourish. But maybe we could have stalled this terrible end, and I wouldn't have been born into a time when there were no good choices left to make.

It's a selfish wish. I know it's my duty to walk toward the scent of blood and wreak the chaos that might allow our survival. But if the world were different, I would gladly turn away from the slaughter.

I know if I survive long enough to leave this place, I'll lose that desire.

The carnage will call to me, and I will run toward the violence, craving the feel of blood on my tongue.

But for now, my mind is my own, and I am glad I have enough human left in me to hate the tasks that lie ahead.

See you in the embers,

~C

CHAPTER THIRTY-THREE

Meet me in the Salt Dome 7:30 tonight.

The message from Alec popped up on my tablet during our morning lesson. My heart did a little swoop that distracted me from the anxiety filling my chest.

I needed a plan. I needed a way to draw out the murderer before they came after me. I needed to keep Mari safe, and to make sure the domes didn't find out the truth about us, and to do a hundred other things, but I wanted to meet Alec. To just melt into his arms for a few minutes and forget how useless I was.

I waited until our class was being herded to the Tropics Dome to type a quick message back.

See you then. Stay safe.

Ignoring Gideon, who still looked like he was in shock, I made my way to Walsh's side.

"Can you come over tonight?" I said.

He gave me a sideways glance.

"I need you to watch Mari," I said. "I have to be somewhere."

"Are you sure it wouldn't be safer for Harper to watch Mari and me to go with you?" Walsh whispered.

"I'll be fine," I said. "Mari can make you dinner."

"Is that all that's making you jumpy?"

"Nope. I'll tell you tonight."

"I love surprises."

I spent the rest of the day trying to think of a way to make my stupid plan work without getting killed or having the domes dig deep enough into my file they'd find out I didn't belong.

We had to be careful. Even Gideon's status wouldn't protect him if things went wrong. But we had to do something. The Dome Guard might be pretending there wasn't a murderer living inside the glass, but I couldn't afford that luxury.

That night, I sat at the dinner table, smiling for Mari as I tried to clear my thoughts enough to really listen to what she'd done that day. But I couldn't stop running through everything in my head over and over again, searching for a better plan.

Maybe, if I'd grown up in a world where kep guards were actually meant to help people, I would have had the sense to stand down and let the Dome Guard do their job, even if it looked like they were just sitting on their asses doing nothing.

I'd have left finding the murderer to them and focused on my schoolwork and the fact that I was supposed to go back into the guard training program in the morning. But I didn't trust the kep, so I kept thinking through options as I washed the dishes and needled Mari into making something special for Walsh.

By the time he came to watch Mari, I'd gone through it all in my head enough times to know even Jaime would agree with my plan. It might not work, but at least it was a good start. And if anything went wrong, the fallout would be small enough we should all be able to walk away unscathed.

"Can I have a minute?" Walsh nodded for me to go out into the hall.

"I'll be back soon, Mar." I gave her a kiss on the head, brushing my hand against the knife hidden on my hip before stepping out into the hall with Walsh.

"Think you need to protect yourself from me?" Walsh whispered after I'd closed the door.

"No. I also don't think I'd stand a chance against you with a kitchen knife, but some habits die hard, especially when there's a boogie man hiding in the shadows."

"You're right, there is someone hiding in the shadows, so why the hell are you separating from Mari to go see Gideon? As good as I am, I can't watch you both at once if you're in different domes."

"I'm not going to see Gideon." I tucked my hands into my pockets to keep from fiddling with my hair. "I'm going to see Alec."

"Tell me you have a good reason for it."

"He sent me a message and asked me to meet him. I'm not sure why, but if I don't go soon, I'll be late."

"This isn't about whatever plan you and Gideon cooked up, is it?" Walsh furrowed his brow.

"I doubt it, but that doesn't mean he won't have something useful to add."

"You do realize out of all of us, I'm the one who has experience with these sorts of things."

"I know." I took his hand, the same hand he'd used to poison Strand. "And I do want your help, but I need Gideon's if I want to keep all of us safe."

"Then don't let meeting Alec make you forget the role you need Gideon to play." He didn't say it with any judgment or anger in his voice, but it felt like he had.

"Just keep Mari safe." I walked out of the building, biting back all the things I wanted to yell at Walsh.

He was right. I knew he was.

Sure, there was a chance Alec wanted to tell me something important, but that wasn't why I was going to see him.

You're stupid and selfish.

I paused at the bottom of the steps leading out of Bloom Dome.

He can help. Even if that's not why he wants you to meet him, he can help.

I kept my wrist pressed to the handle of my knife as I walked to the Salt Dome, carefully making sure none of the people I passed would notice the bump by my hip.

The sun had yet to completely fade from the sky, and the lights in the Salt Dome hadn't been turned on. Shadows filled the spaces between the tanks and beneath the walkway, leaving plenty of places for someone to hide.

I moved slowly, listening for any hint of noise beyond the constant humming of the tanks' filters.

I wanted to call out for Alec, but there was something in the shadows that made me too afraid to speak. What if it hadn't been Alec who'd sent the message? What if someone had followed him into the Salt Dome and hurt him?

I crept up the steps to the scaffolding and over the tops of the tanks, giving up on subtlety and gripping the handle of my knife.

A turtle surfaced as I passed the stingray tank. It took a deep breath, as though trying to remind me that I, too, needed air. But my heart raced too fast for me to worry about something as small as needing oxygen.

A shadow moved on the beach, a person pacing back and forth in the corner where Alec had taken me the night of the dance.

Risking a little noise, I hurried down the steps and onto the sand. I squinted in the dim light, trying to make sure it really was Alec I was running toward.

The figure turned around.

"Lanni." Alec reached for me.

The racing of my heart changed from panicked to pleased as Alec wrapped one arm around my waist, holding me close as he used his free hand to brush my hair away from my face, as though checking me for signs of damage.

"Are you okay?" Alec asked.

"I'm fine. Is there a reason I shouldn't be?"

"I've been so worried. I swear I've wanted to come check on you." Alec held me closer. "But I've been on duty for forty-eight hours. Knowing you're in danger and not being allowed to protect you—"

"Shh." I pressed my fingers to his lips. "I'm fine. Not even a whisper of trouble."

I wriggled out of his arms and took his hand, leading him deeper into the shadows.

"Has Captain Pace told the guards anything more about the fire?" I laced my fingers through his. The warmth of his skin against mine eased the tension in my shoulders.

"Not directly. He called a meeting of the older guards, but none of them are saying why. We've doubled the guards on weapons storage and closed off all passages leading from the Arc Domes to the Incorporation Headquarters higher up the mountain."

We stopped right beside the glass, where the metal structure that supported the tanks blocked us from view.

"At least Captain Pace is smart enough to know this isn't over yet."

"Just not smart enough to know who's behind all this." Alec laid his hand on my hip, touching the hilt of my knife. He flipped up the edge of my shirt, looking at my poor excuse for a weapon. "You shouldn't have to carry that."

"Then find me something better."

"You know I'd do anything to protect you. But giving you a weapon would make you a target for the guards, and that would be a lot worse than having one maniac after you."

"I know." I rested my forehead against his shoulder. "Are you back on duty tomorrow night?"

"No." He tipped my chin and kissed my temple. "I can sneak over, guard you and Mari while you sleep."

"I need you before that." I looked into his eyes. His lips were so close to mine that, for a split second, words just drifted out of my mind.

"I'll stand guard outside Mari's classroom if you want me to."

"It's not that." I edged just far enough away from him to make thinking easier. "I need you to come to the atrium tomorrow night. There's going to be a symposium for the teens who are about to leave school."

"A symposium on what?"

"We'll be discussing Dr. Kain's work and its implications for our future. With any luck, we'll lure the firebug out and the guards will swoop in and arrest them. If they even arrest people in the domes."

"Lanni, that's a terrible idea." Alec took my shoulders.

"If you have a better one, I'd really love to hear it. But the only other options I can come up with involve lighting things on fire, which would definitely get me kicked out of the domes, or waiting to be attacked, which would steal the little sanity I have left."

"The Council won't like it. Incorporation citizens don't just organize symposiums to talk about the future. There are proper channels, and—"

"And what?" I took Alec's face in my hands. "Young people shouldn't show interest in the work of the dearly departed doctor? Young people shouldn't discuss how to fulfill the mission of the domes without treating women like human incubators?"

"What?" A little wrinkle appeared between Alec's eyebrows.

It hadn't occurred to me that he might not know about Kain's work.

"The breeding plans Kain proposed are beyond cruel." I turned away from him, pressing my hands to the glass. "I don't blame the killer for planting the bomb or wanting Kain dead. I've tried to see the people in here as something more than kep, but that woman was a monster. She got what she deserved."

Alec wrapped his arms around my waist. "I'm sorry this isn't the paradise it should be."

I leaned against him, melting into the comfort of his strength. "I knew the Incorporation was a special sort of evil, but I didn't expect kep to look at their women like we're animals."

"We're not all like that. I am not the Incorporation. Neither is Harper or even Captain Pace. The people inside the domes are forced to live by the Incorporation's rules. It doesn't mean we're not smart enough, or compassionate enough, to see that some of the decisions the Incorporation's made are terrible, no matter the justifications they've tried to feed us.

"A few people have been so corrupted by power and distracted by creating an impossible utopia, they've lost sight of the fact that there are human beings inside the glass. Actual people who have to live out whatever terrible plans the Incorporation creates. But I promised I would keep you safe, and that means protecting you even from my own people."

I took his hands, wrapping his arms around me even tighter, like I could wear his sureness as armor.

He kissed the side of my neck. My heart hitched in my chest, and a sigh escaped my lips. He trailed his kisses to the nape of my neck. A tingle ran down my spine, and for the first time, I was glad my hair had been cut short so that soft place could be so easy for his lips to reach.

I let go of his hands, giving him free rein to explore whatever part of me he wanted. But I wanted to kiss him. I wanted to hold him close to me.

I turned around, claiming his mouth. He pressed my back against the glass, trailing his fingers under the edge of my shirt, along the arc of my hip, and to the small of my back.

My body hummed, and all reason disappeared.

I wanted him. I wanted to make him mine and not let anyone else touch him ever again.

I untucked his shirt from his pants as he moved his hand up my side. His thumb grazed the bottom of my ribs as he teased his way closer to my breast.

I unfastened the top of his pants, needing to escape into him before reality overcame desire and the thousand reasons this was a horrible idea came crashing down on us.

"Gideon." I hated myself as I said his name.

Alec froze.

"I kissed Gideon."

CHAPTER THIRTY-FOUR

Alec didn't shout or storm off. He only pulled far enough away to hide the proof that his body didn't really care who I'd kissed as long as I was willing to let him keep touching me.

It seemed like an eternity had passed before he finally spoke. "Why?"

"I needed his help getting some information. I had to convince him I was worth helping."

Alec slid his hand out of my shirt. "Why didn't you ask me?"

"Gideon's dad is the Captain of the Outer Guard. His mom is a doctor. I knew if he tried hard enough, he'd be able to find what I needed."

"So you gave him a kiss." Alec's jaw tensed.

"It was more than one kiss." I eased my hands away from Alec's pants. "But I didn't let it go any further than it had to. I have to protect Mari. I didn't have any other choice."

"Asking me for help would have been another choice. Asking him as a friend would have been another choice. You didn't have to let him touch you." Alec pushed away from me to lean against the metal column that supported the tanks. "There is always another choice."

"That's so easy for you to say." Anger ate through my guilt. "You've spent your life knowing where your next meal would come from. Knowing where you'd find water to drink. Knowing perfect Amery had your fucking back." Tears burned in my eyes. "Not all of us are lucky enough to get to choose how they want to survive. I've never been given any choices."

"You could have at least tried." He dragged his hands over his hair like he was trying to get rid of the feel of my skin.

"Letting Gideon grope me offered the best chance of survival so, no, I didn't have a choice." I swiped the tears from my cheeks. "You should still come to the atrium tomorrow night. If the killer decides to slaughter us all, you won't want to miss your chance to swoop in and save me. Can't let Amery down."

I started to walk away, but Alec caught my wrist.

"Gideon still thinks you're together?" he asked.

"I need his help."

"But do you need him? Do you want him?"

"No." I looked up toward the top of the dome, trying to keep more tears from escaping my eyes.

"Do you still want me?"

"Yes." Pain pinched in my chest.

"Promise you'll end it with him." Alec drew me toward him. "As soon as we find out who's behind all this, you end it with him for good. And if you need something else, you at least give me a chance before going to him."

"You couldn't have—"

"This isn't the outside. It's not all snap decisions and trading whatever it takes to make it until morning. I want to be with you, Lanni." He caressed my cheek and dug his fingers into my hair. "Not just hiding in the shadows. I want to be a part of your life. I can't do that if you're running into Gideon's arms to solve your problems. Give me a chance to be the one you count on. Please."

You don't have to be alone, Jaime whispered in my mind.

"Okay." I leaned against Alec's chest, tucking myself into his arms. "I'll come to you. I'll break things off with Gideon as soon as we're safe."

Alec kissed the top of my head.

We stood quietly for a moment. The sound of his heartbeat pulsed in my ear.

"Walsh is in my room with Mari right now," I said.

"Do you need to get back so he can go?"

"He's spending the night." I looked up at Alec. "He slept in my bed last night while I slept with Mari. I wanted the extra protection."

Alec looked through the glass. "Did you—did you have to bargain for him to stay?"

"No. He didn't ask me for anything." I kissed the side of Alec's neck. "He's just one of the three people in here I actually come close to trusting."

Alec tightened his arms around me.

"I'd ask if you want to stay, too, but I think having both you and Walsh sneak out my window might be a little much."

"Then send him home. I'm an Outer Guard. I'm better trained to protect you."

I teetered on the edge of telling Alec the truth about Walsh. But Walsh's secret wasn't mine to share, and his mission was bigger than either of us.

"Swapping you out would give more people a chance to see I had boys spending the night in my room." I rose up on my toes to kiss Alec's cheek. "Besides, you just got off duty. You need rest."

"I need to make sure you and Mari stay safe." He brushed his lips against mine, delicately, like he wanted to see if something between us had cracked.

"For Amery or for you?"

His body tensed. "Both."

"You haven't heard from him, have you?"

"He has to be careful with what he says. He might be waiting to gather more information before risking reaching out to me."

I buried myself in his arms, trying to stop the panic in my chest from building.

"Lanni, I'm sorry. I swear I will keep trying to get more information."

"Please don't give me any hope. I know you mean well, but I think we're both smart enough to know why Amery's staying quiet."

"If he were dead or someone had found out about him, I'd have heard."

"But if he were grieving for my mom, he'd"—I swallowed the pain in my throat—"he'd need time to figure out how to tell the kids he never knew that he let their mom die. If she's dead, it's because he failed. He didn't protect her."

"What can I do? How can I help you?"

"Can you just hold me for a while? Not talk, just hold me."

"For as long as you want." He tightened his arms around me, holding me close like he could shield me from all the horrors of the world.

I pressed my cheek to his chest and clung to him like he was the last hint of safety left as the world exploded.

He didn't mention the tears that trailed slowly down my face, or try to calm me when my breath hitched in my chest.

When the pain ebbed enough for me to be able to fool Mari, I kissed him one more time and left him in the shadows of the Salt Dome, promising myself that soon he'd be able to walk me home and kiss me where people could see, and I'd never even have to think about letting anyone else touch me ever again.

CHAPTER THIRTY-FIVE

I remember everything about Jaime. The sound of his voice, the way he bent forward when he laughed, his crooked smile, the feel of his hand on my waist when he tucked me close to his side like he knew that was where I belonged.

I don't remember as much about my mother. She wanted me to keep my hair long. She worried about everything. She smiled for Mari but never for me. She was always gone.

I'm not sure if I lost the details of her because she wasn't around enough for me to notice the small things, or if I erased the details from my mind out of spite.

Even now, I'm not sure how much about my mother I actually know. She wrapped herself in so many lies.

I can forgive most of it. Not because she was protecting me, but because I understand I would go to desperate lengths, sacrifice everything, tell any lie, to protect Mari.

I just wish I had someone who could offer me one real, complete truth about my mother.

She couldn't have been gone all those nights just meeting Amery. Did he know what she was doing in the darkness when she wasn't with him? Or was she really just hiding from Mari and me, pretending to sell pleasure in the shadows so I wouldn't question where all of Amery's gifts had come from?

If I had to pick out one thing I knew about my mother and bet my life that I was right, I'd say I was sure she'd do anything to protect Mari and me. Let them use her body, give up any hope of saving herself.

She sent Mari and me to the Arc Domes to protect us and give us a future free from suffering.

I blame Amery for that. He lied to her.

If she'd known how the Incorporation wanted to use us, she would have known we'd be safer on the outside.

CHAPTER THIRTY-SIX

I kept my breathing even, pushing past the stitch in my side that screamed at me for spending so long wasting my time recovering from the fire.

The same guard ran at the front of the pack of trainees, but he pushed us faster than he had before, keeping up a pace that made me glad I had to stick to the back of the pack.

Walsh ran just in front of me and Gideon just behind, like they were guards who'd been assigned to defend me. We hadn't even spread the word about the symposium yet, and it already felt like the walls were watching me, waiting for death to strike.

Mari's safe. Everything will be all right.

I'd sent Harper and Mari to Miranda's for an early breakfast. Between the two of them, they could keep Mari safe. I could have asked Alec to go over, too. But that would have meant risking Gideon seeing Alec. I couldn't afford to lose Gideon's help. Not until after the symposium. Maybe longer if our desperate plan failed.

Gideon shifted to run beside me as we reached the stairs. He looked to me, giving me a nod.

I didn't know what the nod was supposed to mean. Solidarity?

Our plan was a go? He knew how close I'd come to having sex with Alec in the Salt Dome and approved of my deciding Alec was the one I needed holding me if I was supposed to survive in this glass prison?

My steps faltered as we reached the flat level of the corridor that led to the bay.

Gideon grabbed my elbow, steadying me, holding on for a few steps until I'd caught my stride again.

"Thanks," I panted.

Walsh tipped his head a bit, like he'd heard me speak. He turned around, cutting back to run beside me, sandwiching me between him and Gideon.

"I'm really fine," I puffed. "Just got my feet tangled."

That's when I heard the rumble of engines from up ahead in the bay.

The guard leading our pack turned, circling his hand in the air as he sprinted alongside the wall to reach the back of our group and guide us the other way.

"What's going on?" I looked to Gideon.

"Nothing good."

The guard led us down a side corridor, out of view of the bay doors, before stopping. He planted his hands on his hips and took two deep breaths before speaking.

"Change of plans," the guard said. "The Outer Guard are heading to the city this morning, and that includes me. Avoid the path from the barracks to here to keep out of their way. You're dismissed."

"What's going on in the city?" Elliot asked.

The guard didn't answer as he strode through our group and toward the barracks.

"Gideon, what's going on?" Elliot rounded on him.

The whole pack clustered around Gideon. He stepped closer to me, like he wanted to make sure the clump centered on us instead of just him.

"I have no idea," Gideon said. "Dad was eating breakfast with Mom when I woke up this morning, and Paul was still asleep upstairs when I left the house."

The thumping of boots carried from down the hall, heading toward the bay.

"What sort of emergency would call the guards to the city?" Tricia asked.

Walsh glanced toward me as I tensed, like some part of the wolf inside him sensed my urge to scream.

"Whatever it is, there's nothing we can do about it," Gideon said. "There's miles of mountain between us and the city. We're safe here. We can't get there. So let's follow orders and go home."

I took Gideon's hand, squeezing hard enough to make him look at me.

"But I did have something planned for tonight if you're interested," Gideon said.

"Another dance?" one of the boys I didn't know asked.

"More like a symposium," Gideon said.

The flicker of enthusiasm that had rolled through the group faded.

"I know it doesn't sound great." Gideon spoke quickly as a few of the pack started to walk away. "But if you have any interest in your future procr—I mean, happiness—"

"He means sex," I said.

Everyone froze.

"Yes." Gideon blushed. "That. I didn't realize the implications of Dr. Kain's papers until I looked at her work again after she died. The program she proposed could have a profound impact on our lives. Who we're supposed to marry. What the conjugal expectations will be." His cheeks darkened to a bright red. "I'll be in the atrium by the red trees tonight at six."

"Meet by the pond," Walsh said. "Going into the trees will make it look like we're hiding. We want good lines of sight."

"Why?" Tricia asked.

"Because we're going to be talking about the future of the domes," Walsh said. "We're talking about protecting ourselves and the people we care about. If we try to hide what we're doing, we'll risk people ignoring the implications of Dr. Kain's work until it's too late."

"I don't get what the big deal is," Elliot said.

"Go look at her papers and you will," Gideon said.

"We should spread the word," Tricia said. "If it's really that bad, more people should know."

"Yeah." Gideon gripped my hand until my fingers hurt. "Just try and keep it off the adults' radar. Once our peers know what Kain said, no one will be able to stop the knowledge from spreading, but if they ban us from talking about it—"

"Then the information will get removed from the servers," Tricia said. "See you at six."

We all had to head the same way down the hall, but no one spoke. It was like we'd made some silent agreement. Even the few who'd looked skeptical didn't say anything.

I didn't like having a sense of solidarity with so many kep, but I needed them to stand with me if we were going to make this a big enough deal for our plan to work.

Some of them would go tell their parents that we were meeting in the atrium, but that was what we needed. Word to spread far enough for the killer to hear, but not so quickly that the Domes Council would decide to step in and stop us.

My stomach started shaking with nerves. It was stupid. I'd been in plenty of dangerous situations without my gut rolling like I'd be sick, but meeting in the atrium sent fear zinging through me.

You're losing your edge. The domes are making you soft.

I wanted to go find Alec and make him hold me and tell me I was still strong enough to survive on the outside. But he would be loading into a truck right now, ready to ride through the miles of tunnel to reach the city.

"Harper." I yanked free from Gideon's hand and started running.

"What's wrong?" Walsh chased after me.

"If the guards are going, the drivers are going," I said. "Harper was with Miranda watching Mari."

"Shit."

"Go," I said. "You can beat me to her. Just go."

Walsh sprinted away, running faster than I'd ever seen him. I wanted to scream at him not to hold back, but I couldn't ask him to expose what he was when I wasn't even sure there was a problem.

"Do you want me to call for the Dome Guard?"

I hadn't even noticed Gideon running beside me.

"I don't trust them." Wasting air on speaking made my lungs burn.

"Is she with Miranda?"

"That's not enough." I pushed my legs as hard as they would go. The air scoured my throat, making me fight to drag in every breath.

"Slow down!" an older man shouted at me as I tore past him.

I didn't listen.

The corridor leading to Bloom Dome had started to fill with people getting an early start on their workday. Gideon stayed right on my heels as I weaved through them.

She's okay. I bolted up the steps and into Bloom Dome. *She'll be okay.*

I kept repeating it in my head, having to convince myself with every step that I wouldn't be too late and that my little sister would be all right.

There were no flashing lights or alarms in Bloom Dome. Everything seemed peaceful and normal.

The fountain bubbled like normal. The birds soared overhead like normal. There was no smoke tainting the air I fought so hard to breathe.

Miranda's house came into view. The front door was open.

"Mari." I tried to shout her name, but I didn't have enough air left.

Walsh stepped into the doorway. "She's fine. She's here. Everything's fine."

My legs gave out, and I crashed to my knees.

"She's okay." Gideon sank to the ground beside me, shaking and covered in sweat.

"Lanni." Mari squeezed around Walsh to get through the door and tossed herself at me, knocking me backward onto the path and pummeling the tiny amount of air I'd managed to drag in back out of my lungs. "Are you hurt?"

"I'm fine." I coughed, pushing Mari's hair away from her face to make sure she really was okay. "I'm fine, Mar. I was just worried about you."

"I wanted to come to you when Harper had to go, but Miranda said it was better for me to stay here." Mari scrambled off me.

"She was right." My arms shook as I sat up. "You were safer here. But we're both okay, so let's go get ready for school."

"It doesn't ever seem right, does it?" Mari furrowed her brow.

"What do you mean?" Walsh asked.

"That normal things like school have to happen even when everything is going wrong." Mari grabbed my hand, hauling me to my feet. "If the outside is bad enough for all the guards to leave, and the inside is bad enough Miranda couldn't let me go down to get to you, I shouldn't have to sit in a classroom, but I do."

"Yeah, you do." I wrapped my arm around Mari's shoulders, walking her back to our home. "Life keeps going even when it shouldn't. And if we tried to make life stop every time things go wrong—"

"Then we'd always be stuck standing still," Mari said. "I know. But it still doesn't feel right. My stomach gets mushy and squirmy, and I hate it."

"I think that means you're smart," Gideon said.

I hadn't noticed he'd been walking next to us. I glanced back.

Walsh kept four steps behind us, his gaze darting from side to side like he sensed something wrong besides Mari's squirmy gut.

"It takes empathy to know things aren't all right even if you're comfortable," Gideon said.

"More like experience," Mari laughed. She sounded like an adult. A thirty-year-old adult who'd survived too many days on the factory floor.

I pulled her closer to my side. "Let's just get ready for school."

Gideon stepped ahead of us when we reached our building to hold the outside door open. "Do you want me to wait here? I can deal with going to school sweaty."

"You don't have to do that." I herded Mari inside.

"I really don't—"

"Lanni, stop." Walsh's harsh tone sliced a shock of fear up my spine.

I grabbed Mari by the shoulders, pinning her to the wall behind me as Walsh pushed past us toward the door to our room.

"Gideon, take Mari outside." Walsh stopped in front of our door.

"Lanni?" Gideon said.

"Go." I picked Mari up and handed her to Gideon. "Don't leave her."

Walsh stood, one hand raised toward our door, not moving until Gideon and Mari were gone.

"What is it?" I whispered.

"I smell blood." Walsh opened the door.

We couldn't lock our room from the outside. We only had a deadbolt we could turn when we were inside our room. The Incorporation in their utopia-creating pride hadn't prepared for murder and arson, so our door wasn't damaged.

Maybe I imagined it or was just reacting to the tension in

Walsh's shoulders, but I could feel something was wrong before I could even see into our room.

"Shit."

Everything in the closet had been tossed into a pile on the floor. The mattresses had been turned over. The kitchen cupboards were open, and everything had been shifted around. But nothing had been broken, like the person who'd searched my room wanted to be sure they didn't make enough noise to draw any attention.

"Why would they do this?" I picked my way through the pile of clothes to reach the bathroom. "We don't have anything that's not dome-issued."

The room spun as the ground seemed to drop out from under my feet.

"Do they know?" I grabbed the wall, needing the support to hold myself up. "Did someone find out about Mar and me?"

"Unless you've done something stupid, no." Walsh crouched beside Mari's bed, sniffing the bedframe. "Someone cut themselves on the metal. Why bother tearing apart your room when it was obvious you weren't here?"

"My tablet for school." I dove into the closet, reaching into the back corner. "I always tuck it away. Just a habit from before."

"A smart one."

My tablet wasn't in the corner where I'd left it. I knelt, digging through the clothes on the floor.

"Was there anything on the tablet people shouldn't see?" Walsh searched under the scattered clothes.

"No. I'm not that careless. I just use it for school. And..." I shut my eyes, burying my face in my hands. "And I looked up all of Dr. Kain's work. I downloaded her papers."

"Dammit." Walsh paced the tiny space in our kitchen.

"This doesn't change anything."

"Of course it—"

The sound of heavy bootfalls came down the hall.

I scanned the room, panicking about all the things I should hide, but I didn't have any contraband.

Bang. Bang.

The door swung open before the Dome Guard could knock a third time.

"I received word there's been trouble." She stepped into the room, scanning the mess that surrounded me.

"Someone came in and stole my tablet." I didn't bother standing up.

The guard frowned.

"On the plus side, they left some blood behind," Walsh said. "Any chance of you matching it to all that DNA you have stored in your system?"

CHAPTER THIRTY-SEVEN

Showers weren't a thing in the city. There was never enough water to be wasted on that sort of luxury. If you were lucky, like Mari and me, you had enough water to wash from a bowl. When the rains came, you could stand on the roof and scrub just as soon as the smoke and ash had been cleared from the sky.

I'd never known any different. It had all seemed normal to me. But my time in the Arc Domes had softened me, made me used to the privilege of being clean. So, I sat in Captain Tate's office, waiting to find out who'd ransacked our room, trying to ignore the sweat still sticking to my skin.

Gideon, Walsh, and Mari offered plenty of distractions from the way my hair clung to the back of my neck.

Gideon sat in the chair beside me, his leg shaking in a rhythm that made my head pound. Walsh paced by the door, like he wanted to be sure he was mid-motion in case he had to pounce on whoever came to check on us next.

Mari hummed to herself as she sat by my feet, sketching on the tablet one of the guards had given her to keep her busy.

If Mari had been in our room. If I had left her there alone...

But you didn't. You're not that dumb.

"Do you think they'll bring us lunch soon?" Mari looked up at me.

"They will," Gideon said. "If the next person who comes in doesn't have food, we'll remind them we need to eat."

"How long does it take to run a DNA sample?" I stood and started pacing the side wall, keeping out of Walsh's pacing path.

"They already know who it is." Gideon dragged his hands over his hair. "You could tell from the look on Tate's face the last time she came in here. Drawn, nervous. She'd gotten news, and it wasn't something she liked. My guess is we're dealing with a Dome Guard gone rogue."

"Makes sense," Walsh said. "The killer would need access, training. Building a bomb to do just the right amount of damage isn't easy."

"Dome Guard aren't taught how to build bombs," Gideon said.

"They're taught how to recognize what explosives can do," Walsh said. "It's only a small leap from understanding to building. She'd have all the knowledge necessary to figure it out."

"She?" I froze.

"Who has the most to lose from Kain's paper?" Walsh said. "Maybe I'm wrong, but a woman makes the most sense to me."

"So, if they know who *she* is, how long could it take to find her?" I touched my hip, wishing I'd had a moment to grab a knife before the guards Gideon had called came storming into my room.

"If she wants to hide?" Gideon said. "Days."

"What?" My voice echoed around the room.

"Don't panic," Mari said. "They can bring us more meals than just lunch."

"You know what would be a smart idea around here? Security cameras." I pressed my hands to the wall, leaning my weight into my palms like that could somehow draw out the excess energy burning through my limbs.

"The Incorporation values its citizens' right to privacy," Walsh said.

"I don't think Kain would've agreed." Gideon stood to pace the wall opposite me. "We've got to get out of here before six. We can't miss the symposium."

"We planned the symposium to draw out the killer." I stepped away from my pacing wall. "If the guards know who's responsible for all this bullshit—"

"It doesn't change anything." Gideon dragged his hands over his hair again. "It's too late to cancel."

"Can't you just send some messages to the people we've talked to?" I said.

"I mean I refuse to cancel." Gideon gripped the top of his head like he wanted to rip his own thoughts out. "I'd never actually understood Kain's plan. I knew about the DNA bank, and the theory of why we needed it, but what Kain proposed, it's inhumane."

"You think?" Walsh shot Gideon a glare but didn't stop pacing.

"I had never read her papers until I knew I was supposed to lead the symposium," Gideon said. "If I never had, you can bet ninety percent of our class has no idea that Kain proposed—"

"A whole new kind of hell." I cut across him, glancing toward Mari, who sat leaning back against the desk, watching all of us prowl without a hint of fear on her face.

"We need to make sure Kain's papers stay theoretical, and the best way to do that is to make sure our peers understand what they'd be getting into if the Incorporation decides to follow the path Kain laid out," Gideon said.

"Do you really believe the Incorporation cares what a bunch of teenagers think?" I asked.

"We owe it to ourselves to try." Gideon glanced down to Mari. "We owe it to the ones who come after us. We can't"—he shut his eyes, like he was trying to measure his words—"I will never forgive myself if we just sit back and let this happen."

"But do we need to do this now?" Walsh said. "Give us a year, we'll be out of school. We'll have more control."

You'll already be gone, and I'll still be locked in here.

I dug my nails into my palms, swallowing the words I wanted to scream at Walsh. "Some of us don't have the privilege of waiting for our problems to solve themselves."

Walsh met my gaze for a moment. I wished we could read each other's minds.

"Stand with me on this one, Walsh," I said. "I've had your back. Now you have mine."

"So how do we get out of here?" Walsh said.

"We wait for them to catch the person who wants us dead," Mari said. "We'll get to go home after that."

"And if they don't find them in the next few hours?" I asked.

"You sneak out." Mari shrugged.

"There are two guards outside the door," Gideon said.

"Do I get to punch them?" I asked.

"I'll just scream and cry really loud and all of you can go to the atrium," Mari said.

"What?" I knelt beside my sister.

"It's what Harper would say to do," Mari said. "I'll make a big fuss like I'm traumatized because someone left blood on my bedframe, and then you can go without punching anybody. Miranda might be a little fussed about it, but she'll probably just feed me and braid my hair to make me feel better. I can scream and cry really loud. I promise."

"Your sister's useful," Walsh said.

"And if they haven't found the killer yet, you're staying in here with her," I said.

"You want to go to the atrium without me?" Walsh finally stopped pacing.

"No. I'd feel a lot better if you came with me, but I have to know Mari is safe. Please, Walsh."

He stared at me for a moment before nodding.

"Great. We have a plan." Gideon bounced on his toes. "What do we do for the next few hours?"

"It's called waiting." Walsh started pacing again. "And it's awful."

A guard brought us a tray of food and some bottles of water. The rumble of a pack of guards running down the hall came three times. Twice going north. Once going south.

I lay down on the floor and closed my eyes, trying to convince myself to relax. There was nothing I could do. There were guards stationed outside our only exit.

Trapped. Trapped in a concrete box.

Panic zapped through my chest. I got up to pace some more.

Mari curled up under Tate's desk and fell asleep. Part of me hoped she could sleep because she felt safe since I was watching over her. Part of me wanted to scream at her, yell until she understood she should never have that much faith in one person.

You have to trust somebody.

I closed my eyes, savoring the sound of Jaime's voice in my mind.

"Will we know when the Outer Guard get back?" I asked.

Walsh gave a tiny nod.

I wondered if he'd be able to hear them returning.

"Probably," Gideon said. "If they called everyone out there, something big is going on. There'll be at least a few wounded. They'd have to pass this way to get to the medical corridor."

"What do you think is happening out there?" I sat beside Mari.

"Who knows?" Gideon said. "Last time they called everyone out, they had to do a house-to-house search. Do they have Vamp where you're from, in the city by the Ice Domes?"

"Yeah," Walsh said. "We have vampires."

"None of the people in our city are allowed to chemically alter their bodies," Gideon said. "Dad had gotten word that some

Vamp had made it into the city, and they had to weed out the dealers before the drug could spread."

"How'd that work out?" Walsh asked.

"They found two dealers and a dozen Vampers," Gideon said. "We lost an Outer Guard, but it kept the population of the city pure."

"Do you think they'll be back before six?" I asked.

"Probably not." Gideon grimaced. "It's for the best. If the Dome Guard are busy and the Outer Guard aren't here, we might actually have a chance of getting through to people before anyone tries to stop the symposium."

"Stop us how?"

"No idea." Gideon slid down to sit against the wall. "I've never tried to publicly speak against the Incorporation."

"I'm sorry I got you into this." I got up and went to sit beside him.

"Don't be." He laced his fingers through mine and kissed the back of my hand. "Better to speak up now than to have to fight back when they're trying to haul you into a sterile room."

A wave of nausea swept through my stomach.

"We'll make sure that never happens." He put his arm around my shoulders, pulling me in to lean against his side. "Not to you. Not to Mari. We'll stop it before it starts."

CHAPTER THIRTY-EIGHT

I need you to believe me. I know my purpose was never to help the people who have gained so much through the Incorporation's violence. I understand my place.

But it's not only outsiders the Incorporation is willing to torment. I've copied out a passage from one of their doctor's proposals for the future of the domes. I needed to memorize it so I would never forget how deep their evil extends. I wish you could see it too, so I could prove I haven't forgotten all the harm they've done to us, even as I begin to pity them.

Should the male participant still be living, the most efficient course of action would be conception through intercourse. A sterile room should be provided in the medical corridor where the sexual act can take place. The female's ovulation cycle must be carefully tracked so she can be bred quickly. She should be taken to the room for mating twice daily until conception occurs.

In the event of unwilling participants, females can easily be sedated for the copulation process without causing harm to the fetus. The necessary medication for unwilling male participants will require further consideration—phosphodiesterase inhibitors will be needed. The correct dosage in *combination with sedatives must be calculated on an individual basis. Should both parties be unwilling, more forceful means of ensuring compliance will be implemented.*

I would have torn their throats out if they'd tried to put you in a sterile room against your will. I would have killed them all to defend you. I would have slaughtered anyone who tried to drug me and put me in a room, too. We would have fought back.

Even after all they've done to break us, we wouldn't have silently walked into that kind of hell. But the people inside the glass have lived so surrounded by evil, they don't know what it looks like when their fellow monsters turn on them.

I'm afraid some of them will submit without question.

I hope the ones who fight back will destroy the Incorporation from the inside out.

Let the monsters slaughter each other. I would be grateful to have less blood on my hands.

See you in the embers,

~C

CHAPTER THIRTY-NINE

At 5:46 p.m. the Dome Guard still hadn't found whoever it was they were looking for.

I'd paced, braided Mari's hair three times, wished I still had long hair of my own so I wouldn't have to take my anxiety out on my little sister's scalp.

Mari gave up on playing with the tablet and drew invisible pictures on the floor. From the way she pursed her lips, she had a definite image in mind. I wished I could see whatever picture it was that kept her so focused.

At 5:48 p.m. Mari sighed and brushed her hands across the place she'd been drawing. "Should I just scream really loud, or should I pretend to sob really hard and you can call for help?"

"You should sob," I said. "If you scream, they might think one of us tried to hurt you."

"Right." Mari stood and balled her hands at her sides.

"Wait." Walsh stepped toward me. "Lanni, can we talk?"

"Sure, let's go for a walk and have a little chat," I said.

Walsh frowned and beckoned me to follow him toward the corner of the room.

"Be right back." I joined Walsh to huddle in the corner, all of five feet from Gideon and Mari.

Walsh leaned close to my ear to whisper. "Don't go up there with him. The last thing you need is to get on the Incorporation's radar any more than you already are. The Dome Guard are after the killer. Once they find them, you and Mari will be safe."

"Safe from a murderer, not from Dr. Kain's ideas," I whispered back.

"Let Gideon talk to people about Kain's work," Walsh said. "You don't need to be there."

"Yes, I do." I took Walsh's hand. "I need to make sure the others understand how bad things could get in here."

"Lanni—"

"You have an exit strategy. Mar and I don't. We're stuck in here for good. I have to protect my sister. I can't let her grow up to be abused worse in here than she would've been back home."

Walsh closed his eyes for a moment before nodding.

"Keep her safe." I squeezed Walsh's hand and stepped away.

Mari and Gideon sat beside each other on the front of Captain Tate's desk. Neither of them looked happy about Walsh and me whispering in the corner.

"Okay, Mar. You're up."

She nodded a few times before screwing up her face and giving the most pathetic blubbering wail I'd ever heard.

"It's okay, Mar." I spoke loudly, directing my voice toward the door. "I promise, everything's going to be all right."

"No it's not." Mari coughed out a sob. "We're locked in, and I don't feel good. My belly hurts so bad I think I'm gonna be sick."

I almost laughed out loud as Mari clutched her stomach. She'd survived life in the city and only gotten sick enough to vomit once.

"You're just upset." I crept toward the door. "Take some deep breaths, and everything will be okay."

"Not it won't!" Mari shouted. "We're going to be stuck in here forever, and I don't feel good."

"Okay. Okay. I'll see if I can get you a snack."

Mari started screaming and sobbing at the same time. The high pitch of it all dug into my brain and froze me on the spot as my instinct to run from the sound battled with my need to comfort the one making it.

"I'll get some help." I reached for the door, barely leaping back in time to avoid being hit in the face as the door swung open and our two guards came bursting in.

"What's going on?" The female guard approached Mari while the male stayed in the doorway, blocking my escape.

"I"—Mari gasped—"don't feel"—she coughed like she was gagging on her words—"I don't feel good." She crumpled to the ground, her cries suddenly going quiet in a way that made my heart stop.

"Mari." Walsh ran toward her. "Mari, you have to breathe." He turned her onto her back.

She flopped over like she'd passed out.

"We need medical," the female guard said.

The male guard stepped farther into the room, staring at Mari like she was some weird, lethal animal as he spoke into the band on his wrist. "Alert medical we need assistance in Captain Tate's office. We have a child who's collapsed for unknown reasons."

"She's breathing," Walsh said.

A hand closed around my wrist.

I glanced up to find Gideon dragging me toward the door. I let myself look at Mari for one more moment before following him into the hall.

We kept to a fast walk, quick enough to be out of sight before the guards who were tending to Mari realized we were gone, slow enough not to look like we were running away.

"I feel like a shit for leaving her," I said.

"Don't," Gideon said. "But make sure you congratulate her on an excellent performance."

"Mar has had—" A shock tightened my throat. I couldn't tell Gideon that Mari had used the cute and innocent kid act to get me out of trouble more than once. "She's always been a little dramatic."

"She's lucky to have you, you know." Gideon took my hand as we started up the first set of stairs heading toward the atrium.

"Miranda's better with her. She cooks more, braids her hair better."

"None of that really matters. If the Incorporation decides to institute Kain's plan, you'd protect Mari. What do you think Miranda would do?"

"Tell Mari how wonderful it is that the Incorporation figured out how to make sure the Arc Domes would be filled with kids." I laced my fingers through Gideon's, needing to feel his palm pressing against mine to keep my mind from spinning into the panicked place where breaking through the glass and taking Mari out into the wilderness seemed like the only way to protect her.

"Wait." Gideon tugged on my arm, keeping me from reaching the next level as the thudding of someone running in heavy boots came toward us.

We walked down a few steps, keeping our backs to the passing people. I glanced up in time to see three Dome Guard tearing down the corridor.

"I hope that's a good thing," I said.

Deep. Deep. Deep.

The sound echoed through the stairwell.

Deep. Deep. Deep.

"What does that mean?" I tensed, waiting for something to explode.

"My guess is the Outer Guard are back and things didn't go well in the city." Gideon steered me back up the stairs. "That sound means all doctors and support staff are to report to the medical corridor."

"Don't doctors have wrist bands with coms?"

"Yes. But the cleaning crews don't." Gideon's jaw tensed. The muscles in his neck turned into strained ridges.

Alec.

We ran up another flight of stairs, farther from where the medical staff were gathering.

"Do you need to go down to medical?" I asked.

"Why?"

"To check on your dad and brothers."

We cut down a corridor and to the steps to the atrium.

"I wouldn't be allowed to see them anyway." Gideon peered up toward the next level before climbing the stairs. "I'm not a doctor. I'm of no use down there. We just ran away from Tate's office to do this. We're not missing our chance."

I grabbed his wrist with my free hand, slowing him down as we neared the top of the steps. There were people in the atrium. I could hear their voices over the soft sounds of the water. None of the voices sounded mad or like they were giving orders.

We stopped in the entrance to the atrium. I scanned the trees, searching the shadows for any hint of someone waiting to jump out and stab me.

I need a weapon. I need Walsh.

As we cut back toward the pond, a disgusting feeling of self-loathing twisted my stomach. I didn't want Walsh to be in the atrium for comfort or support. I wanted him there so I could use him as a weapon. If I was willing to use him to kill, was that really any better than the Incorporation wanting to use women to breed?

"Don't get nervous," Gideon said. "I know I have to do all the talking. You shouldn't even stand next to me."

"This was my idea."

"And I have a completely clean record. If someone is going to get in trouble for speaking out, it needs to be me."

The pond came into view. Thirty teens had gathered by the water. Some looking tense, like they understood why they were there. More lounging around, like they were just waiting for another dance to begin.

"Stay safely in the group where no one can get to you." Gideon kissed the back of my hand.

"Gideon, I'm sorry for dragging you into this."

"Don't be. I'm just glad someone opened my eyes before it was too late."

"Gideon what's all this about?" a boy I didn't recognize asked as we reached the back of the group.

"Are they sending more people to another set of domes?" a girl asked.

"Let him through." Elliot waved people away, clearing our path.

We reached the edge of the pack near the pond, and Gideon let go of my hand.

I hated him standing in front of everyone alone. I hated that he had his back to the water even more. I should have stood behind him, protecting him as he dared to speak against the monsters of the Incorporation.

But I just stood with the rest, watching as he took a deep breath before speaking.

"We all know Dr. Kain and her family died last week," Gideon said. "What the Domes Council has tried so hard to keep quiet is that the Kains were murdered. All three of them stabbed before their home was burned."

A murmur of disbelief fluttered through the crowd, like the world had been too kind to all of them and having a murderer in their home was too horrifying to be believed.

"And I think I know why," Gideon pressed on. "I read through Dr. Kain's published papers. The plan she proposed for procreation in the domes is nothing short of criminal."

The murmurs in the group got louder.

"If the Incorporation were to follow Dr. Kain's plan, we would see husbands and wives separated, forced to mate with people they didn't choose." Gideon spoke over the crowd.

"But we have to protect the genetic diversity in the domes," a girl said. "If we don't—"

"There is a difference between protecting genetic diversity and drugging people to force them to have sex," Gideon said. "What Dr. Kain proposed was nothing less than rape. Incorporation-approved, mass rape."

Someone behind me gasped. I glanced back. One of the girls had tears streaming down her cheeks as she clung to the boy beside her.

"This could start with our generation. This isn't hypothetical. We've lost too many guards. We sent dozens to the River Domes. The attack at the depot cost us the new guards who were supposed to transfer here," Gideon said. "We have to stand up for ourselves. We have to make it clear to the Council and to the Incorporation itself that none of us will allow ourselves, our spouses, or our friends to be abused in the pursuit of Dr. Kain's agenda."

Shouts came from the crowd.

"We won't let them!"

"How can we protect each other?"

"What can we do?"

Gideon raised a hand, calling for quiet. "Dr. Kain is dead. But she outlined her proposed breeding program before she was killed. Whoever murdered her did nothing to stop her theory—"

"It's not a theory." The woman's voice was strong and determined. Loud enough to make us all look away from Gideon and toward the trees to the left of our group.

A woman in a black uniform stepped out of the shadows. She held a black box with a blinking light in one hand and a gun in the other.

CHAPTER FORTY

The woman waited as the horde screamed and a few fools scattered.

Elliot made it twenty feet before she shot him in the neck. He crumpled to the ground. I didn't know if she'd used a lethal dart or if he'd only been tranqed.

The rest of the group drew back together, huddling into a tight knot like they were all eager to use the people around them as living shields.

"No one wants to hurt you." Gideon shifted to stand between the woman and the rest of our pack. "We only came here to make sure that what Dr. Kain proposed doesn't happen to anyone."

"You're too late." The woman moved closer to us, clutching the black box to her side.

"What do you mean *too late?*" I stepped up to stand next to Gideon. I couldn't leave him alone. I wanted to run, or hide behind the pack, but I couldn't bring myself to abandon him.

"The River Domes." The woman's voice shook, like she could barely say the words. "They'd lost so many people to the violence in their city. They sent our guards there to stop the vampires.

That's what they said. To stop the vampires and make the River Domes safe."

"But they didn't come home," Gideon said. "All the Outer Guard we sent were killed."

"It's so much worse than that!" She aimed her gun at Gideon's chest. "They took my husband. They sent him away to protect, to defend. He knew what he was getting into. He knew he could die. But the River Domes didn't have enough children. They needed more children. And our guards were there."

A horrible cold filtered into my chest. "They made the guards breed."

"He was my husband." She pointed her gun at me. "He was my husband, and they said he couldn't come home unless he had sex with that woman. He had to get her pregnant if he wanted to come back to me. The Council hadn't even cleared us to have a baby. They made him get her pregnant before I ever even got a chance."

"And then he died," I said.

"The guards should have come back sooner. They should have made it home. But the Incorporation was using them like disposable whores. Abusing them. Defiling their bodies." Tears slid down the woman's cheeks. I hadn't realized how young she was until that moment. She couldn't have been more than twenty-three. "Because of Dr. Kain, I don't have a husband anymore."

"I'm so sorry." Gideon stepped sideways, planting himself between the gun and me. "What the Incorporation allowed to happen—"

"What they forced to happen!"

"What they forced to happen," Gideon said. "We're trying to make sure it never happens again. We want to be sure no one else ever faces the abuse your husband suffered. That no one feels pain like yours ever again. That's what you want, right? To make sure this stops?"

The woman laughed, choking on her tears.

"That's not it." I stepped around Gideon, needing to watch the woman's grip on her gun. "You don't want to stop it from ever happening again. You want to make sure the people who hurt him pay for what they did to you."

"You're smarter than I thought you'd be," the woman said.

"We're not the ones who hurt him," I said. "None of us had anything to do with what happened to you."

"We all understand that what the Incorporation did to your husband was wrong," Gideon said.

"You don't," she said. "Your father let it happen. He was their captain. He should have protected them. If I kill you, he'll find out what it feels like to lose someone he loves."

"Don't!" I planted myself in front of Gideon. "You don't want to go down this path. You'll never make it out of this atrium."

"Move." She inched closer to me.

"If you start running now, you could still have a chance," I said. "You're a Dome Guard. You must know some way you can sneak out."

"Get out of my way. I don't want to hurt you." She aimed her gun for my neck. "You're the only person here I can't blame. I wanted to. I wanted to hate you. I wanted to destroy you. You shouldn't have run into that fire. It was my revenge, not your chance to be a hero."

"She was only trying to—"

"I'm not a hero," I cut across Gideon, desperate to keep the woman focused on me.

"I dove so deep into your life, looking for the perfect way to make you suffer, but there's nothing. I couldn't believe it. You don't belong here. How did you do it? Your records are perfect. Everything so well done, I thought I'd lost my mind."

The cold in my stomach sharpened into fear.

"I even went into your room, trying to figure it out," she said. "Not a trace from before. Where did you come from? Who are—"

I leapt forward, ramming my forearm against her wrist, knocking the gun from her hand.

I barely heard the pop of the gun going off as it fell to the ground. I punched hard, aiming for her throat. She stumbled back. The black box slipped from her grip.

Everything seemed to slow down as the box fell.

Someone grabbed my arm, yanking me back. Weight landed on top of me, crushing the air from my lungs as a bang shook the atrium.

I felt the heat of the explosion and heard the screams of the people around me. But I didn't feel any pain.

I lay still for a moment, waiting for agony to sear through my torn limbs.

A cough rattled in my ear. Blood dripped onto my face.

I twisted sideways, trying to push away the weight that held me down.

The person on top of me gave a groan that turned into another blood-dripping cough.

I slid my forearm under my chest, using all the leverage I could manage to roll the person on top of me off my body.

He screamed.

"Gideon." I scrambled to my knees.

He had blood around his mouth. He coughed, and more blood came out.

"We need a doctor," I shouted. I didn't know who I was talking to. "We need a doctor!"

A watery gurgle came from Gideon's throat, like he was drowning in his own blood.

"Okay, we need to stop the bleeding." I took Gideon's hand. "I think I need to roll you back onto your stomach. I think that's right. Should I put you on your stomach?"

He blinked at me. His eyes started to close.

"Gideon. Gideon!" I looked around, searching for someone in a white jacket who could tell me what to do.

The woman was...gone. They'd have to run her DNA if they wanted to prove who she'd been.

Some of the others were on the ground, bleeding, even though they'd been farther away from the explosion than I had.

"You protected me." I squeezed Gideon's hand. He didn't move. "I'm going to roll you over. I have to see what's wrong. I'm sorry."

I took Gideon's shoulder, rolling him onto his stomach.

Blood covered his back and the backs of his legs. There were too many small wounds to count. I didn't know which of them was making him cough blood.

"We need help!" I screamed. "Somebody has to call for help!"

I ripped away the torn remains of Gideon's shirt and caught a glint of metal sticking out of his skin.

"I can't take it out. If I take it out, it'll make it worse."

Heat streamed down my face. I pressed the back of my hand to my cheek, trying to find where I'd been wounded. I found tears instead.

"Shit. We're going to need more medical aid in the atrium." Captain Tate ran toward me, speaking into the band on her wrist. "We have at least three critically wounded. If Pace is mobile, get him up here. His son looks bad."

"He needs help." I got to my feet, staggering as the trees around mc tipped. "Gideon needs help."

Dome Guard streamed toward us.

Two doctors in white coats followed behind.

"Over here," Tate called to one of the doctors.

I stepped away from Gideon, giving a doctor room as she shouted orders to the guards.

"What happened?"

They loaded Gideon onto a long stretcher. The doctor spoke into the band on her wrist.

"Miss Roberts, what happened?" Tate stepped in front of me, blocking my view of Gideon. "Who did this?"

I pointed to the bits of the woman the blast had left behind. "She had a gun and a bomb. I got the gun away from her. Her husband was sent—"

Tate walked away, moving onto the next crisis now that her domes were free from danger.

They carried Gideon away.

It looked like he was still breathing. I couldn't really tell.

I searched the ground, trying to find someone to help, but the Dome Guard were already seeing to everyone who'd been injured.

"Are you bleeding?" a woman with dark eyes like my mom's asked.

"I don't think so." I reached up to touch my cheek. My hand was covered in blood.

The guard circled me. "There's blood on the back of your leg."

I looked down. Some metal had found its way into my calf.

"I'll be fine," I said. "My sister can dig it out for me."

"We need to stop the bleeding and get you down to the medical corridor," the guard said.

"It's a scratch." I headed toward the stairs. A flare of pain sliced into my leg.

"You need medical attention." The guard gripped my shoulders like she thought I might tip over.

"I'm fine." I shrugged away from her. "My sister is in Tate's office. I'll go straight to medical from there."

"You're bleeding," the guard said.

"Not that badly. Help someone else."

The guard didn't follow me to the stairs.

I could feel pain in my leg, but it didn't seem bad enough to make it so hard to get down the steps. It was like my ankle couldn't figure out how to work anymore.

"Clear a path!" someone shouted from above.

I pressed my back against the wall.

Two guards carried a stretcher past. It was Tricia. She wasn't moving.

Gideon had been so determined to make sure everyone knew about Kain's work. If all of them died, it would have been for nothing.

Corpses can't reshape the future.

By the time I reached the second flight of stairs, I could feel my blood in my shoe. Other people's blood had marred the corridor, too.

It had to be from the atrium. The Outer Guard wouldn't have been on these stairs.

Alec had gone out into the city. Outer Guard had been hurt. I didn't know if he was okay.

Gideon had been hurt. I didn't know if he'd survive.

I walked with one hand on the wall as I went down the last set of stairs to the bay and medical level, heading straight for Tate's office. The injured had spilled out of the medical corridor.

Gurneys had been set out in the hall just beyond Tate's office. Guards and doctors moved between patients.

I couldn't see Gideon.

They're helping him. They just didn't make him wait in the hall.

I didn't let myself consider that he might already be dead.

I needed to get to Mari. I had the ability to protect her. There wasn't anything I could do to help Gideon.

I hugged the wall, staying out of the way of the stream of patients coming down from the atrium. When I reached Tate's office, I tried to open the door, but it wouldn't budge.

"Mari." I banged on the door. "Mari!"

"Lanni!" Mari shouted from inside the office. "Are you okay?"

"I'm fine, Mar." Tears burned in my eyes.

"They got mad when you left, so they locked us in," Mari said. "We're okay, though."

"Good." I sank to the ground. "That's all that matters."

"What happened?"

I pictured Mari with her cheek pressed against the door.

"Don't worry about it right now." I ripped the sleeve from my shirt and tied it around the wound on my calf. "You're safe. We can worry about everything else later."

I scooted into the doorway, out of the path of the guards, and propped my bloody leg up against the doorjamb.

"Have there been injuries?" Walsh asked.

"Yeah." I shut my eyes, focusing on the growing throbbing in my leg.

"Gideon?" Walsh asked.

"Yeah."

CHAPTER FORTY-ONE

I don't know how long I slept for, or how I'd even managed to fall asleep with all the chaos in the corridor.

"Lanni." Someone spoke softly, like how Mom used to wake me up when I was little. "Lanni."

A hand squeezed my shoulder.

I opened my eyes, trying to get my gaze to focus on the face hovering just above mine.

"Lanni, where are you hurt?" Alec asked.

I blinked again, making sure it really was him.

His face was gray from fatigue and streaked with dirt and dried blood.

"Alec." I moved to reach for him and gasped as pain shocked from my hurt calf to my spine.

"Careful." Alec eased a hand behind my back, helping me sit up. "Where are you hurt?"

"My calf." I winced as I lifted my leg down from where I'd propped it against the doorjamb. "I think everything else is just sore. Are you okay? They said the Outer Guard had been attacked."

"We were." He brushed my hair away from my face. "But I'm okay. We need to get you to a doctor."

"Other people need help more."

"They've already gone through most of the injured. Let me carry you over."

"I can't leave Mari and Walsh. They're locked in."

"Everyone on the Council has been called up to Incorporation Headquarters." Alec scooped me into his arms. "No one else is going to have a key to Tate's office. And we can't let you sit here wounded while you wait for Captain Tate to come back."

"I can't leave Mari locked in there." I pushed against Alec's chest.

"If you let a doctor look at your leg, I'll see what I can do about getting a key to let them out. Deal?"

I chewed my lips together. I'd pissed Tate off. Alec had survived an attack in the city. He had a better chance of getting a key.

"Deal." I let him carry me down the hall even though I could've made it on my own two feet.

Having Alec hold me close made all the people lying on gurneys in the hall seem less like a nightmare that would swallow me whole and more like another awful day I could survive.

The gurneys stopped when we reached the medical corridor proper. But the smears of blood staining the floor and sounds of sharp orders coming through the closed doors were almost worse.

Alec carried me into a room at the end of the hall. Five beds had been set up. A pile of linens poured out of the hamper in the corner.

"More?" A young man strode into the room behind us. "Put her on the far bed. We have to keep patients in order in case we have another disaster."

Alec laid me down on my assigned bed.

"I'm really fine. I just have some metal in my calf," I said.

"Shrapnel is never fine." The doctor shined a bright light into my eyes.

"Have you heard anything about Gideon Pace?" I asked.

"Last I heard, he was in surgery," the doctor said. "Seems like he was the worst of the wounded from the atrium."

"He protected me." Heat burned in my eyes. "Isn't there anything you could be doing to help him instead?"

"No." The doctor tucked his light into his pocket. "Lie on your stomach."

I lay down, hating putting myself in such a vulnerable position.

Alec held my hand as the doctor cut the sleeve I'd used to bandage my leg and sliced away the bottom of my pants.

"Doesn't look like the shard is too big," the doctor said. "We should be able to pull it out without surgery."

The band on the doctor's wrist began to beep.

"What's happening now?" Alec tensed, reaching for the gun on his belt.

"I'm needed in another room. Don't move." The doctor bolted back into the corridor.

We sat quietly for a minute. Someone down the hall screamed in pain.

"Are you sure you're okay?" Alec kissed the back of my hand where I hadn't managed to coat my skin in blood.

"Yeah." I pulled him closer to me so I could feel his arm pressing against mine. "The killer is dead, but I'd really like to be done with explosions. Never seeing a bomb again would be great."

"Yeah. It would." Alec's eyes darkened, like he was drifting away into the shadows.

"What happened out there?" I twisted my wrist, taking my turn to kiss the back of his hand.

"It doesn't matter."

"Yes, it does." I pushed myself up onto my elbows, ignoring the ache in my spine. "Tell me."

"Our briefing said a few Vamp dealers and up to twenty vampires. We were going in during the day to ambush their shelter. It just all went wrong."

"How?"

"They had explosives. They'd rigged the street to blow right over a fuel line. It was like the depot all over again. Just fire scorching through everything."

"I'm so sorry." I tightened my grip on Alec's hand.

"We finally broke through to their nest." Alec wrapped an arm over the back of my waist and leaned close to my ear. "They weren't vampires. But I don't know what they were. We busted out the roof, they should have sun burned, but it didn't bother them. I've heard rumors of other altered humans, but these were—"

"Werewolves." I twisted to sit up, needing to be facing the door. "You went into a den of werewolves."

Alec kept an arm behind me, like he knew damn well the screaming in the back of my mind had started again as the color of the blood on my hands sharpened, like my body wanted to be sure I didn't miss the danger creeping in around me.

"I don't know what kind of monsters they were," Alec said. "The way they fought, it was like they enjoyed feeling our blood on their hands. I wish I'd never seen that kind of violence, but I keep going through it in my head. Planting bombs near fuel sources. Having altered people who can move in the sunlight. We've seen it before. The attacks are too similar. I think their group followed us from the depot. Attacked there and made their way to the city on the other side of the mountain. It just makes too much sense."

"I need you to get to Mari." I pulled Alec's arm out from behind me. "You have to get her out of Tate's office. She's not safe in there."

"Even if I'm right, there are dozens of levels of security between the city and here."

"Get to Mari." I shoved him toward the door.

"What's wrong?"

"You have to protect her. Walsh isn't—" I couldn't make myself say it. Not even to Alec. Not even with wolves at our door.

"Lanni?"

"He isn't an Outer Guard." The words seemed like they were coming from far away instead of my own mouth. "He doesn't understand what's happening in the city. If the alarms go off, Mari can't be locked in with only him to protect her. Alec, go. Please."

Alec kissed my forehead and ran out into the hall.

Everything around me seemed to buzz as the horrible reality of the coming battle crashed into my chest.

I'd lived my life in a world full of monsters. If the time had come for the demons to fight each other, I wouldn't be the one to stop the war.

But I had to protect Mari. I had to get her out.

No matter what her freedom cost.

Lanni's journey continues in Eye of Stone.

CHAPTER ONE

Nola dug her fingers into the warm dirt. Around her, the green-house smelled of damp earth, mist, and fresh, clean air.

Carefully, she took the tiny seed and placed it at the bottom of the hole her finger had made.

Thump.

Soon the seed would take root. A sprout would break through to the surface.

Thump, bang.

Then the green stem would grow until bean pods sprouted.

Bang, thump!

The food would be harvested and brought to their tables. All of the families would be fed.

"Ahhhhh!" the voice came from the other side of the glass. Nola knew she shouldn't look, but she couldn't ignore the sounds any longer.

It was a woman this time, her skin gray with angry, red patches dotting her face. She slammed her fists into the glass, leaving smears of red behind. The woman didn't seem to care as she banged her bloody hands into the glass over and over.

"Magnolia."

Nola jumped as Mrs. Pearson placed a hand on her shoulder.

"Don't pay her any mind," Mrs. Pearson said. "She can't get through the glass."

"But she's bleeding." Nola pushed the words past the knot in her throat.

The woman bashed her head against the glass.

"She needs help," Nola said. The woman stared right at her.

Mrs. Pearson took Nola's shoulders and turned her back to her plant tray. "That woman is beyond your help, Magnolia. Paying her any attention will only make it worse. There is nothing you can do."

Nola felt eyes staring at her. Not just the woman on the other side of the glass. The rest of the class was staring at her now, too.

Bang. Thump.

Families. The food she planted would feed the families.

Bang.

Pop.

Nola spun back to the glass. Two guards were outside now. One held his gun high. A thin spike protruded from the woman's neck. Her eyelids fluttered for a moment before she slid down the glass, leaving a streak of blood behind her.

"See," Mrs. Pearson said, smoothing Nola's hair, "they'll take her where she can't hurt herself or any of us ever again."

Nola nodded, turning back to the tray of dirt. Make a hole, plant the seed, grow the food. But the streaks of blood were burned into her mind.

The setting sun gave the greenhouse an orange-red gleam when the chime finally sounded.

"Students," Mrs. Pearson called over the sounds of her class packing up for the evening, "remember, tomorrow is Charity Day. Please dress and prepare accordingly. Anyone who doesn't come ready to leave the domes will be sent home, and their grades will be docked."

"Thank you, Mrs. Pearson," the students chorused as they drifted down into the hall.

"Magnolia."

Nola pretended she hadn't heard Mrs. Pearson call her name as she slipped in front of the group leaving the greenhouse. She didn't want to be asked if she was all right or told the sick woman would be cared for. And she didn't want to see if the glass had already been wiped clean.

Lights flickered on, sensing the group heading down the steps. Hooks lined the hallway, awaiting the gardening uniforms. Nola pulled off her rubber boots and unzipped her brown and green jumpsuit, straightening her sweater before shrugging out of the dirt-covered uniform. The rest of the class chatted as they changed—plans for the evening, talk of tomorrow's trip into the city. Nola beat the rest of them to the sink to scrub her hands. The harsh smell of the soap stung her nose, and the steaming water turned her hands red. But in a minute, the only sign of her time in the greenhouses that remained was a bit of dirt on the long brown braid that hung over her shoulder.

"Nola." Jeremy Ridgeway took his place next to Nola at the sinks, shaking the dirt from his light brown hair like a dog. It would have been funny if Nola had been in the mood to laugh. "Are you ready for tomorrow?"

"Sure. It's our duty to help the less fortunate." She sounded like a parrot, repeating what their teachers said every time Charity Day came around. Nola turned to walk away.

Jeremy stopped her, taking her hand.

"Are you okay?" Wrinkles formed on his forehead, and concern filled his deep brown eyes.

"Of course." Nola forced herself to smile.

"Do you want to come over tonight?" Jeremy asked, still holding her hand. "I mean"—his cheeks flushed—"my sister and my dad are off-duty tonight, and she hasn't seen you in a while."

"I've got to get home. My mom leaves tomorrow. But tell your dad and Gentry I said hi." Nola pulled her hand away and half-ran down the hall. More lights flickered on as she sped down the corridor. She made herself breathe, fighting her guilt at running away from Jeremy. She liked being in the greenhouses better than the tunnels that dug down into the earth. There might only be a few feet of dirt on top of her, but knowing it was there pressed an impossible weight on her lungs.

The hum of the air-filtration system calmly buzzed overhead. The solar panels aboveground generated power so she could breathe down here. She pictured the schematics in her head. Lots of vents. Great big vents. The air would be filtered, cleaned and purified, and the big vents would bring oxygen down to her.

Blue paint on the wall read *Bright Dome* above an arrow pointing to a corridor on the left. Nola ran faster, knowing soon she would be aboveground. In a minute she was sprinting up the steps. She took a deep, gulping breath. The air in the tunnels might be the same as the air in the domes, but it felt so different.

The sun had set, leaving only the bright lights of the city across the river and the faint twinkle of the other domes to peer through the glass. Nola squinted at the far side of Bright Dome. The other homestead domes glowed gently, but if she tried, she could almost make out a few stars. At least that's what she told herself. It might only have been wishful thinking.

Tall trees reached almost to the roof of Bright Dome. Grass and wildflowers coated the ground around the stone footpaths that led from house to house. Nola followed the path through the buildings to the far side of the dome. Twelve families shared Bright Dome, each of them lucky enough to have been granted independent housing units.

The trees in the dome hung heavy with crisp, green leaves. The flowers had begun to close their petals for the night. A squirrel darted past Nola's feet.

"A little late getting home, buddy." Nola's pulse slowed with each step closer to home.

The birds were all flying back to their nests. Bright Dome had been assigned robins and blue jays this cycle. The birds and the squirrels shared their home to be kept safe from contamination. The domes provided them all protection from the toxic air and tainted water.

The lights were on in Nola's house as she swung open the door.

"Hey, Mom," Nola called.

"Mmmhmm." The sound came from her mother's office in the back of the kitchen.

"How was your day?" Nola pulled the pot of steaming vegetables from the stove, knowing they would be overdone without having to lift the lid.

"Fine," her mother said, running her fingers through her shoulder-length, chestnut hair, which had been graying quickly of late. "We've been running samples in the lab all day."

"You'll figure it out." Nola didn't ask what the problem in the lab was. Her mother, Lenora Kent, was one of the heads of the botanical preservation group. It was their job to decide what plants from the outside needed to be preserved and how to take care of those plants once they were safely inside the domes. Whatever her mother was working on was for the good of them all. Beyond that it was all vague answers about classified projects.

Nola pulled bowls down from the cabinet, dishing out steamed beans and broccoli, adding spices to make the food taste like something real.

Nola pushed the bowl in front of her mother. Only when she put the spoon in Lenora's hand did her mother seem to notice Nola was still in the room.

"How was your day, sweetie?" Lenora looked up at her daughter.

Nola's mind flashed to the woman. Pounding on the glass, shattering the serenity of the greenhouse.

"It was fine." Nola smiled. "Don't forget to pack for the conference. It'll be colder at Green Leaf, so pack your sweaters."

"Of course." Lenora nodded, but she was already looking back at the charts on her computer screen.

Nola carried her dinner up the narrow stairs to the second floor. She crept into her mother's room and found the duffel bag under her bed. Nola pulled clothes out of the tiny closet. They were lucky. The residents of the domes hadn't been forced into uniforms outside of work and school. Yet. That would come when there was no one left on the outside to work in manufacturing.

When she had counted out enough blouses and slacks for her mother's week-long trip, Nola moved the suitcase to the head of the bed, where her mother would have to see it if she went to sleep that night. A picture in a carved wood frame sat on the nightstand. Six faces beamed out of the photo. A ten-year-old version of herself sat in a tree above her mother and father. Kieran sat on the branch next to her, and below him were his parents.

Nola touched her father's face, wishing the photo was larger so she could properly see his bright blue eyes that had matched her own. But her father was dead, killed in the same riot as Kieran's mother. And now Kieran and his father had been banished from the domes. The photo blurred as tears pooled in Nola's eyes.

She slid the picture into the top of her mother's bag. Lenora would need a bit of home during the Green Leaf Conference— even if their family had broken.

Nola snuck across the tiny landing at the top of the stairs and into her room. She climbed straight into bed, leaving her dinner forgotten on her desk. She pushed her face into her pillow, hoping sleep would come before the face of the woman desperate to get through the glass.

Order Girl of Glass *to continue the story*.

ALSO BY MEGAN O'RUSSELL

<u>The Girl of Glass Series</u>

Girl of Glass

Boy of Blood

Night of Never

Son of Sun

<u>The Tale of Bryant Adams</u>

How I Magically Messed Up My Life in Four Freakin' Days

Seven Things Not to Do When Everyone's Trying to Kill You

Three Simple Steps to Wizarding Domination

Five Spellbinding Laws of International Larceny

<u>The Tethering Series</u>

The Tethering

The Siren's Realm

The Dragon Unbound

The Blood Heir

<u>The Chronicles of Maggie Trent</u>

The Girl Without Magic

The Girl Locked With Gold

The Girl Cloaked in Shadow

<u>Ena of Ilbrea</u>

Wrath and Wing

Ember and Stone

Mountain and Ash

Ice and Sky

Feather and Flame

Guilds of Ilbrea

Inker and Crown

Myth and Storm

Serpent and Steel

The Heart of Smoke Series

Heart of Smoke

Soul of Glass

Eye of Stone

Ash of Ages

www.ingramcontent.com/pod-product-compliance
Lightning Source LLC
Chambersburg PA
CBHW021125190726
48288CB00008B/2496